Murder in Ashville

A Samantha Degan Mystery
by
Jane O'Brien

Copyright 2017 by Jane O'Brien

For information, email **Cozy Cat Press**, cozycatpress@aol.com or visit our website at: www.cozycatpress.com

COZY CAT
P R E S S

ISBN: 978-1-946063-18-2

Printed in the United States of America

Cover design by Paula Ellenberger
www.paulaellenberger.com

1 2 3 4 5 6 7 8 9 10

A special thank you to my family: my son, John, who started me on the path to publishing my stories; my son, Tom, who thinks it's great his mother is an author; my daughter, Christine, who sings my praises and buys my books; and my husband, Dave, who wholeheartedly supports my efforts and shares his computer with me. I love you all.

PROLOGUE

Samantha Degan, the author of the best-seller, *Memoirs of Professor Fenwick Stonehill*, mystery writer, and sometime sleuth, was on her way to her hometown of Ashville. She was struggling to keep her mind on the road because of the conversation she'd had with her mother the day before.

Think of the wedding, she told herself. *The wedding is my own. I'm marrying Detective Joseph Fletcher next week.* Detective Fletcher, known as Fletch, was the love of her life. Thinking back, she knew she'd fallen in love with him even before he slapped handcuffs on her wrists, and arrested her for Professor Stonehill's murder. Not only was she innocent of the crime, she and Fletch had discovered the real culprit together.

Now she was on her way to Ashville alone. Fletch wouldn't arrive until next week, because he had limited vacation time since his partner, Detective Robin Wells, was on maternity leave.

Although Robin was a new mother to an infant, her parents would be sitting with the baby and two older boys while she and her husband, Frank, attended the wedding. Megan Fairchild, Samantha's friend and assistant, and her boyfriend, Mike, were the maid of honor and the best man.

Samantha and Fletch's mothers were supposed to be arranging a simple wedding for the couple. However, from what Samantha had gathered through conversations with her mother, Colleen Degan, the wedding was becoming anything but simple. Samantha didn't want to dampen her relatives' enthusiasm, but was afraid they were getting carried away. She planned to arrive in Ashville early to help with the wedding and pull on the reins, if necessary.

Samantha and Fletch hadn't been apart for more than twenty-four hours since the day they met. There was an ache in her heart thinking about how much she missed him, and they'd been together just one hour ago.

It would be good to see all her high school friends. She hadn't been home for any length of time since graduation. School and working part-time jobs had kept her in Lancashire for the last few years. The day she began working for Professor Stonehill was a turning point in her financial woes. Not only did he pay her well, but she was given a beautiful room in his mansion and three meals a day. With this income, she was able to pay her school expenses and save a little too. He also left her a sizable sum when he died.

Fletch encouraged Samantha to continue to write; his salary would be enough for the two of them, he said, and she didn't even need to think about getting a job. Her hope was that her mysteries would take off and soon she would be able to kick in her fair share.

The closer she came to Ashville, the more she thought about her mother's phone call telling her Patsy Burke had been seriously injured in an automobile accident. She could hear Colleen Degan's words in her ear. *The police suspect foul play.*

Samantha hadn't known Patsy well. She was a quiet, studious girl who always seemed to have her nose in a book. Patsy had called Samantha a few days ago. She was anxious to talk to her privately about C.J. Sinclair's death. She claimed there was reason to believe that his fall nine years ago was not accidental.

Now Patsy could be dying under suspicious circumstances.

CHAPTER 1

Colleen Degan and Sandy Fletcher ran out of the Degan house when they heard Samantha's Volkswagen bug pull into the driveway.

Archie Degan and Jack Fletcher circled around from the garage where they were struggling to put Archie's new charcoal grill together.

Samantha was happy to be home and happy too that her folks and Fletch's were getting along so well.

"When are you going to get rid of that beat up old car?" asked Archie.

"Don't say that, Dad; you'll hurt his feelings," Samantha said in all seriousness.

Jack Fletcher gave her a bear hug; he and Fletch's mother, Sandy, were crazy about their soon-to-be daughter.

Archie carried her luggage into the house while Colleen and Sandy walked with their arms around her.

*****

Colleen poured everyone iced tea and set a plate of cookies on the large table in the country kitchen where Samantha and her brothers had eaten dinner every night when she was growing up.

It's good being home again, but I can't wait until Fletch gets here too, Samantha thought to herself.

After inquiring about her brothers and their families and Fletch's brother and sisters, Samantha asked her mother about Patsy Burke.

"It's a tragedy; I didn't know it until I saw in the paper that Patsy Burke is *Dear Patsy*, the advice to the lovelorn columnist from the *Ashville Tribune*."

"I didn't know the *Tribune* had an advice columnist."

"Oh, yes; it started over a year ago. *Dear Patsy* is popular in our town. There isn't a problem she doesn't have an answer for, and she always does it in a clever and humorous way."

"You said the accident was suspicious; have you heard any more about it?"

"Only that it's under investigation. Dad heard someone cut the brake line on her car. She was driving down from the hills and the brakes failed, the car careened off the highway, and dropped some fifty feet below. She somehow opened the door and fell or jumped out before the car hit the ground. The poor thing. I heard she has a head injury and hasn't regained conscientiousness."

"That's terrible," Samantha said. "I'll stop by the hospital this afternoon to see what I can find out."

*****

Samantha thought it best not to tell her mother about the conversation she'd with Patsy a few days earlier. Her mom wouldn't intentionally gossip but she knew how the ladies of Ashville liked to get together and discuss the happenings in town. The temptation to share the information with her friends might be too great for her mother.

*****

After lunch, and hearing all the details of the mothers' plans for her wedding, Samantha called the small hospital for an update on Patsy Burke's condition. The nurse said Patsy was allowed visitors. Samantha excused herself and drove through town to the hospital.

She'd forgotten how small the town she'd grown up in was. She spotted the ice cream shop on the corner where she and her friends hung out after school. The gazebo in the center of town. The drug store that always carried the latest fashion magazines. She'd devoured those books when she was going through her wanabee fashion designer phase. So many memories were going through her mind. Samantha had spent more time with her friends in high school than she had on her studies. It was fun while it lasted, but she realized after her first week in college, that she wouldn't have time for fun if she was going to make it to her sophomore year.

She drove into the parking lot of the hospital. Other than a new wing on the south end of the building, it looked the same. Samantha remembered, with sadness, spending the last few days of her grandmother's life in the waiting room. She was only eleven when her beloved Gran suffered a stroke and never recovered. Eleven-year-old children were not encouraged to visit hospital patients, but the nurses allowed Samantha to sit by Gran's bedside and hold her hand. Samantha smiled to herself remembering her wannabee nurse phase.

After checking with the front desk, she walked directly to Patsy Burke's room, expecting to see the timid girl with her nose in a book. Instead, a very attractive woman with wavy, auburn hair and carefully applied makeup sat surrounded by papers, writing feverishly.

"Patsy?" Samantha said, thinking she had the wrong room.

"Samantha, you haven't changed a bit. It's been almost ten years and you still look like a teenaged cheerleader."

"Thank you for that, Patsy. You *have* changed; you look terrific. How are you feeling? I didn't expect to see you looking so healthy."

"I've got a hard head; the doctor promised I could get out of here tomorrow if I behave myself today."

"Is it true someone tampered with your car before your accident?"

"That's what the police tell me; they say the brake line was cut. I received a strange phone call earlier yesterday. The voice was low and muffled and the person told me to meet them at Hill Point, that they had evidence proving C.J. Sinclair's accident was murder. I drove directly to Hill Point and waited over an hour and nobody showed up. I finally gave up and started driving down the hill. As my speed picked up, I stepped on the brake. I knew immediately that something was terribly wrong. I heard a snap and my foot went to the floor. I was certain I was going to die when the car headed toward the cliff. I was panic-stricken but managed to open the door and push myself out. I don't remember a thing after that until I woke up in Intensive Care. They tell me I'm lucky because I landed in heavy moss and missed several tree trunks that would have killed me.

"I guess I'm lucky, although my car exploded and there's a possibility someone tried to kill me."

"What questions did you have about C.J.'s accident? You mentioned, over the phone, that it might not have been an accident."

"It started over a month ago. I don't know if you're aware that the *Ashville Tribune* now has an advice column. It's called *Dear Patsy*, and I'm the Patsy. I receive letters all the time, sometimes they're from people who have serious problems and sometimes they're just cranks. I received one that looked strange because it was typed on a typewriter. You just don't see that anymore. All it said was ...*all have sinned*... with the initials *CJS*. I didn't think much about it and filed it away. I keep old letters in a file even though they don't make sense or they're obvious pranks.

"A week later, I received another letter. *...revealer of secrets...* I didn't take it seriously and filed it away too.

"After that, the letters began coming every other day. I began keeping a list of the words when I received the letters... *a lying tongue is but for a moment... do not lie to one another... lying lips are an abomination... he who breathes out lies will not escape...*

"I must have received fifteen letters, all with the initials *CJS*. I decided to take them to the police. They were in my purse as I walked to the parking lot to my car. I felt someone's hand on my shoulder and the next thing I knew, I was on the ground and my purse was missing. It all happened so fast, I didn't know what hit me. There wasn't anyone around to witness the incident.

"My keys were in the purse and I had no way of starting the car. My extra set was at home which meant I'd have to break into the house to retrieve them. I walked back to the newspaper offices to call the police to report the crime. Maggie, the front desk clerk, stopped me. Apparently, someone had dropped off my purse saying they'd found it on the sidewalk. Maggie said it was an older gentleman who walked with a cane. My keys, my identification, my money, everything was in the purse except the letters I was taking to the police station. I wasn't sure what to do. I didn't think the police would be able to do anything about it just on my word that there was something suspicious about the letters. It dawned on me at that point that the initials could stand for C.J. Sinclair. That's when I called you. I thought it could wait until you arrived, but then I received the call asking me to come to Hill Point."

"Have the police interviewed you since the accident?"

"No, my doctor hasn't given them the okay. I wish I had those letters to show them."

"I'd better let you get some rest, Patsy."

"Please don't leave. I feel fine and I'd love to hear all about the wedding and your guy. I heard he's a detective."

Samantha told her friend the story of how she and Fletch had met and the rocky start to their relationship.

"Now, tell me about yourself; what caused this transformation?"

"You noticed," Patsy laughed. "I hope I've changed for the better since high school. I was painfully shy when you knew me. I lived with my mother on the outskirts of town. Mom did her best but there was never enough money for any extras. Thinking back, it was my fault that I didn't have friends; you and some of the others tried to include me in your circle but I was too ashamed of my appearance to join in.

"I found, if I stuck my nose in a book, people ignored me and that was the way I liked it. All that reading did me some good because I was given a full scholarship to a college near Albany.

"On the first day, my roommate, Jenny Davenport, walked into our room and shrieked, 'Girl, what have you done to yourself, or what haven't you done? I can't possibly have a mousy thing like you as a roommate.'

"I was mortified; I didn't know where I'd go, but I began to pack my suitcase. Then Jenny said, 'What are you doing and where do you think you're going? We have work to do. Let's start with that hair.'

"To make a long story short, Jenny transformed me. I felt pretty for the first time in my life and more than that, I felt like I fit in. I was still quiet and shy but after living with Jenny for four years, I finally came out of my shell."

"You do look terrific. I'm glad you feel good about yourself. What brought you back to Ashville and *Dear Patsy*?"

"After graduation, I began working as an intern for the local newspaper. Brad Collins was a sports writer; we started seeing each other outside of work and one weekend we flew off to Vegas and got married.

"We cared for each other, but we had nothing in common. Being a sports writer, Brad attended every game of every sort. What he didn't see in person, he recorded and watched into the wee hours. Mom and I never watched sporting events on television and I never went to any of the high school games. I knew nothing about sports and cared even less."

"The marriage lasted less than two years. We were still friends, but it was awkward working so closely. Mother became ill and it was a good excuse to come home to Ashville so I could be with her during her last few months. I needed a job and Mr. Stanford was looking for someone to write an advice column. It's not the newspaper job I envisioned, but I enjoy it, and in a small way, it fills a need for some people."

"From what my mother tells me, your columns are very entertaining. I'm glad you found something that brings you pleasure. Do you have columns written in advance?"

"Yes, my assistant publishes them daily. Do you remember Amber Beardsley? She's an intern at the newspaper as part of a work-study program through the high school. She's Coach Beardsley's daughter."

"Amber Beardsley? She was just a little girl' I can't believe she's in high school and working too."

"She's a sweetheart; she's interested in journalism. She's a smart cookie and has a good chance of succeeding."

"How is Coach Beardsley? I remember him at C.J.'s funeral; it was the first time I'd ever seen a grown man cry."

"I don't know him well, but Amber talks about him often. Her brother, Josh, is on the junior varsity football team and doing well. There's talk around town that he'll be going pro in a few years. They said the same thing about C.J., didn't they?"

There was a knock on the door and Officer Allison Jennings entered Patsy's room.

CHAPTER 2

Officer Jennings introduced herself to Patsy, saying she had questions for her about the accident if she felt up to it.

"Hello, Allison," said Samantha.

"Samantha, I never expected to see you in this room. I knew you were coming to town for your wedding. I can't tell you how excited we all are for you."

The two women hugged.

"I'd better get going and let you interview Patsy. I'll catch up with you later."

"Samantha, please don't go," said Patsy. "I'd like you to stay if you have the time."

"I can stay if it's all right with Officer Jennings."

"I don't see why not. Wait a minute; are you the Patsy Burke who went to high school with us? I thought you looked familiar, but I couldn't place you. You certainly have changed; you look terrific!"

"Not only that," said Samantha, "Patsy is the famous "Dear Patsy" of the *Ashville Tribune*."

Allison nodded her admiration but needed to get business taken care of. She questioned Patsy thoroughly about the accident and why she answered an anonymous caller's request to meet at Hill Point.

Patsy told Officer Jennings about the letters she'd received and suspected someone was looking for the truth about what had happened to C.J. Sinclair years ago. She also told the police officer about the letters that were stolen from her purse. The purse was found and turned into the newspaper office with everything intact except the letters.

"Why are you bringing up C.J.'s death now? It was a horrible time for everyone. It's finished and that's the way it should be."

"Allison," said Samantha, "Patsy didn't start the conversation about C.J., someone else did. It's obvious someone has information about his death—or for some bizarre reason, they're fabricating a mystery."

"You said an old man with a cane brought your purse to the newspaper office."

"Yes, that's correct, according to Maggie at the front desk."

"It sounds like old Gus. He lives downtown in the boarding house on Seventh and Vine. He walks around town when the weather's nice. Would you object if I brought him to your hospital room?"

"I don't object, but I never saw the man."

"It will make him feel important if I ask him to be involved in the case."

Allison left with the promise of returning before Patsy was discharged.

"What's that all about? Allison acted like she didn't believe me; why would I lie about something like that?"

"Maybe she just wants to be sure to touch all bases. It can't be easy for her being the only female officer in the Ashville Police Department. It's that good old boy attitude, I'm afraid."

******

Samantha didn't intend to spend as much time as she had in Patsy's hospital room. She sensed her friend was more concerned about someone trying to kill her than she let on.

Twenty minutes later, Allison returned with old Gus. She introduced him to Patsy and Samantha.

Looking directly at Patsy, he said: "That's her; that's the one who gave me twenty dollars to take the purse to the newspaper office."

"Gus, we've never met before today. You're mistaking me for someone else."

"I might be old, but I remember pretty faces and I remember your shiny brown hair too."

"Thanks, Gus, you've been a big help," said Allison. "Officer Decker will take you back home now."

*****

"What's your game, Patsy? You talk about letters some unknown person sent to you that suddenly disappear. You fake a mugging; maybe you faked the accident too. Your injuries are minor compared to what should have happened when you jumped out of your car. Did you come back to Ashville to cause trouble? Are you seeking revenge on us because you were a mousy little nobody in high school? Why are you lying about C.J. Sinclair?"

"Allison, that's enough," cried Samantha. "I believe Patsy is telling the truth. You can't take the word of that old man. You brought him here to identify the person who gave him money for doing a job. He walked in here expecting to see that person and he assumed it was Patsy. You knew he wouldn't be a reliable witness."

"Samantha, I know you think you're an ace detective, but this is my territory, so please keep out of it."

"Allison, please calm down, what's gotten you so riled up?" asked Patsy.

"Because C.J. Sinclair is gone and won't be coming back. We don't need some busybody coming to Ashville and rekindling old wounds and destroying our lives."

"I'm not trying to destroy anything, Allison," replied Patsy. "I did receive those letters and someone, obviously, doesn't want me to pursue the matter. No matter what you think, I did not rig my car to cause an accident. I'm not that stupid or brave, and I don't like pain. I'm sorry if investigating what happened that day brings back distressing memories but don't you want to know the truth?"

"Yes, of course, I do. It's just such a shock to be questioning C.J.'s death after so many years. I'm sorry; I'm not acting very professional. The boys at the station would give me a hard time if they knew how I'd lost it."

"We'll never tell, will we, Samantha?"

*****

Officer Jennings left Patsy's room after she'd taken the accident report. She apologized for her earlier comments. Patsy said she understood and they parted as friends.

"You're a forgiving person, Patsy. Some of the things Allison said to you were very unkind."

"She's in pain, I understand that. One thing about being an observer all those years, I knew more about what was going on with the gang than most of you did."

"What do you mean?"

"Did you know that Allison thought she was in love with C.J.?"

CHAPTER 3

Samantha had known C.J. Sinclair since the two of them were toddlers. The Sinclairs lived next door to the Degans and the couples spent many hours together.

C.J. was closer to Samantha's age than he was to any of her siblings, and he was like a brother to her. She knew he was handsome as a teenager, but there was never anything but friendship between them.

He excelled in athletics and school work as well. He was popular with both the guys and the girls. He had everything going for him and then it all ended abruptly when he slipped off a cliff and fell to his death.

Samantha knew he often walked alone and loved climbing on the cliffs over Lake Ashville. She'd admonish him for being a show-off at his nervous mother's expense. He had climbed on those cliffs since he was old enough to ride his bike to the lake. That was why it was so shocking when he was found dead in the shallow waters. It was early spring; the weather was warm and the cliffs were clear of any frost or wetness to make them slick.

The more Samantha thought about it, the more she wondered if someone did, indeed, push C.J. to his death. *Who would do such a thing?* Samantha wondered. *C.J. was loved by everyone, wasn't he?*

*****

She left the hospital so that Patsy could get some much-needed rest. The doctor thought it best that she stay in the hospital one more night. Samantha told her she'd pick her up in the morning and drive her home.

Samantha's mother and Sandy Fletcher had everything under control for the wedding on Saturday. She was grateful to them because the distraction of a possible nine-year-old murder was taking much of her time.

Samantha drove to Hill Point. In the old days, it was the site of an exclusive restaurant. Her parents took her there on her sixteenth birthday. The food was excellent, but she knew it cost her father close to a week's salary. Unfortunately, for the owners, the restaurant was too expensive for most of the folks in Ashville and it closed shortly after her birthday celebration. The building was later destroyed and it became a favorite spot for teenage parties. Samantha had been to a few of those parties herself. She remembered the ride down the hill with a date who'd had too much beer, and she decided she'd stick to parties in town after that.

Riding back down the hill, she could only imagine the fear Patsy must have experienced with no brakes to slow her down. She stopped at the spot where Patsy had jumped from her car. She got out of the car and her stomach turned as she looked to the bottom of the ravine where Patsy's car had landed. Walking toward the mossy area where Patsy made her escape, Samantha could still see the imprint of her body on the damp moss. There was no doubt in her mind that Patsy was telling the truth. She would have risked her life if she'd faked the accident.

*****

Samantha pulled into the driveway of her parents' house. She glanced over at the house where the Sinclairs had lived. After C.J.'s death, his parents had sold the home and moved to South Carolina. Mrs. Sinclair never got over the loss of her son; she passed away five years ago at the age of fifty-seven. Mr. Sinclair married a widow with five grown children and fifteen grandchildren. He's happiest when the large family all get together and the ache in his heart disappears, if only for a little while.

*****

"Samantha, dear, you're home! Jody called; she and Erin are going to stop by to see you shortly. Have you had lunch? I've made egg salad sandwiches with green olives—just how you like it."

"That sounds wonderful, Mom. I'm famished."

Colleen asked about *Dear Patsy* while Samantha ate her sandwich and drank her chocolate milk. She hadn't had that combination since she was in grade school but had to admit, it tasted good.

"Patsy is doing well; they're keeping her overnight but it's only precautionary. As she said, she has a hard head."

"I don't remember her from your school; she isn't one of the girls from your circle of friends, is she?"

"No. Patsy was a loner. She's come out of her shell though; she's beautiful and very self-assured now. I'm sorry I didn't try harder to get to know her back in school. Allison Jennings came by to question Patsy about the accident. Did you know she's a cop?"

"Oh, yes; there was a terrible stink when she signed onto the police department. She's the first female officer the force has ever had. Can you believe that in this day and age? I don't know how they got away with hiring only men all these years. It's a good thing; there are times when a woman's better for the job than a man."

"She seems quite bitter. Do you think it's because people give her a hard time?"

"She was always so cheerful despite her father. He was a miserable old coot. She lost some of that bounce when C.J. died; his death touched all you girls. It was such a tragedy and so senseless."

"I know what you mean; I loved C.J. like a brother. It seems he and Allison were together but I never knew that."

"According to Frances Sinclair, girls called C.J. all the time. She once said it was so bad, they considered getting an unlisted phone number. She wasn't the type to brag about her boy, so I'm sure it was true."

"I know he was popular, but I didn't know my friends were swooning over him," Samantha laughed.

"Here are the girls now. Finish your sandwich and I'll let them in."

Colleen smiled watching the old friends hugging and squealing like in the old days. She was sorry those times were over, but happy to have her daughter home, if only for a few days.

Jody showed pictures of her two little boys. Her husband, Will, was home with them, giving her some time to be with her friend.

"Will sounds like a nice guy; I'm anxious to meet him," said Samantha.

"He is a nice guy; he was there to pick up the pieces after Ted Blanchard broke my heart."

"Ted Blanchard, I haven't thought about him in years. I didn't realize you two were ever together."

"It was after you left for college. He's the biological father of my children. I fell in love with him but he, obviously, didn't feel the same way. I got pregnant the first time and he said we'd get married. He had no intention of doing so. I still lived at home when Mason was born. Ted stopped by to see his son. I was a complete fool and believed it meant he wanted to be a family. Nine months later, I gave birth to Alexander. My parents would have disowned me, but they fell in love with my boys. Then I met Will and everything changed. He treated me like I'd never been treated before. He loves the boys like they're his own. You'd have thought after C.J., I'd have learned to be a better judge of character."

"You and C.J.? I didn't know you two were together. How did I not know that?" asked Samantha.

"I thought you were secretly in love with him and didn't want to hurt you," said Jody.

"For heaven sake," replied Samantha, "C.J. was a friend from childhood. We didn't have romantic feelings for each other. I can't believe you dated him in secret. Allison said the same thing."

Samantha looked at Erin who gave her a sheepish grin.

"You too, Erin?"

"I'm afraid so. C.J. was irresistible. I thought I was too smart to fall for his charms, but I was wrong. I think that's why I'm still single. I've never found anyone to measure up to C.J. Sinclair."

"All this time, I thought C.J. was such a great guy. He seems to have strung you two along with, who knows how many other girls in our class. How could I have not known what a sleaze he was?"

"We all kept it from you and from each other. Erin and I accidentally discovered we were both dating him at the same time. We didn't speak for the second half of our junior year. After C.J. died, we found comfort in each other and have remained friends since."

"We didn't mean to upset you," said Erin. "Why don't we talk about your wedding instead?"

"You didn't upset me; I'm just wondering why I never knew what C.J. was really like."

"Samantha, you always saw the good in everyone."

CHAPTER 4

"Anybody home?" called out Kate Turner, another high school friend. She was standing at the back door. Samantha embraced her old friend.

"I can't believe I'm here with you guys again. It's like the last nine years never happened."

"And we haven't changed a bit," laughed Jody.

"Jody and I were confessing our sinful ways with C.J. Sinclair. Samantha just told us she wasn't in love with him after all."

"I could have told you that," said Kate. "Not everyone in Ashville High had the hots for that guy."

"Of course, you didn't; you only had eyes for Nick Turner."

"Samantha, every time we get together, the conversation always comes around to C.J. I hate to sound cold, but he's been gone for almost ten years now. Can't we let him rest in peace?"

"Let's talk about 'Dear Patsy'," Jody suggested. "Can you believe that mousy little flower finally bloomed? I never guessed Patsy Burke became our favorite advice to the lovelorn columnist. Samantha, have you read any of her answers?"

"I haven't gone through Mom's recycle bin for old papers, but I've heard so much about 'Dear Patsy,' I'll be sure to do it before they get picked up tomorrow. I've never heard of an advice column getting so much attention before."

"She could be a stand-up comic. She's hilarious and has excellent advice to boot. I feel bad that we never reached out to her in high school. I thought we were better than that," said Jody.

"I saw Patsy today," said Samantha. "She seems to understand it was her timidity that put people off. She's really a very nice person. I can't give you the specifics, but she could be in serious trouble. The accident might not have been an accident at all."

"Is that the sleuthhound in you talking, or do you have reason to believe Patsy's in trouble? You've got to stop hanging out with people who end up dead," Kate laughed nervously.

"Speaking of sleuths, when are we going to meet your detective? I'm sure he's gorgeous; you never settled for anyone who wasn't. Remember Bobby Rooney? He's a big shot lawyer in New York City now. Will heard he's considering a run for Congress. Just think, you could have been a Congressman's wife."

"No, thank you; I had my fill of politics when the illustrious mayor of Lancashire's bloodied head fell in my lap."

The mention of Bobby Rooney's name brought back memories for Samantha. Back then she was sure they'd be married someday. Her heart was broken the day he left for college the summer before her senior year. He promised to e-mail and call her every day. At first, she heard from him so often that she left her computer up and running so she didn't miss a word. Gradually, his calls and e-mails came less and less frequently. He told her he was busy with his studies, that college was much more intense than high school. By the end of October of that year, she wasn't surprised to learn that Bobby was involved with someone else. Although she suspected the worst, she was devastated knowing she'd lost the love of her life. Never one to wallow in self-pity, Samantha put all her energy into her studies. She dated during the year, but life was never the same without Bobby Rooney.

Samantha was grateful to whoever the girl was who stole Bobby's heart. If he hadn't dumped her, she might never have met Fletch. She finally knew what real love was and she couldn't wait to be his wife.

"Samantha, Erin asked if Fletch is bringing any of his single friends."

"I'm afraid not; his partner Robin will be here with her husband. She's on maternity leave now and, with Fletch gone too, they can't spare any of the other officers."

"Do you trust him working with a woman?"

"Robin's a good friend to both of us. She has three children and a terrific husband. If I had any doubts about Fletch, I certainly wouldn't be marrying him."

"Jody has a trust issue with men ever since C.J. cheated on her," said Erin.

"Every conversation we ever have circles back to C.J. Sinclair. I don't want his name mentioned in my presence again, do you understand?" said Kate.

*****

As much as Samantha liked being with her childhood friends, she could only take so much of them at one sitting. These three, and Allison too, never got over being teenagers. Maybe it was because they'd stayed in the same small town all their lives. She loved visiting Ashville. All her family had been there their entire lives too. Maybe it was her imagination, but she felt their conversation sounded the same as it had ten years ago.

She wasn't sorry when Jody said she had to get home to the children. Erin drove her so they left together. Kate stayed a while longer and talked about her family. There was no mention of C.J. Sinclair or the accident that took his life.

*****

Samantha was happy when her cell phone rang and it was Fletch.

"It's so good to hear your voice. I miss you so much. That old saying is true, you can't go home again."

"Are the moms giving you a hard time?" he asked.

"The moms have been wonderful. It's my old girlfriends. It makes me very happy I met you and made Lancashire my home. After a few hours with those girls, I feel like I'm back in high school."

They talked until Fletch had to hang up to answer another call. Samantha heard her mother's land line ring while she was talking with Fletch. She didn't think anything about it until her mother popped her head into the kitchen.

"Samantha, dear, you'll never guess who's in town visiting his mother? Bobby Rooney, although he's calling himself Bob now. He said he heard you were in town too and wants to stop by to see you. I told him it would be all right. I hope you don't mind."

"Oh, Mom, I wish you hadn't done that; I was hoping to relax in my bedroom and read one of my old Nancy Drew mysteries. I can't believe you kept them all these years."

"I'm sorry, dear; I'm afraid he's on his way over. You were such good friends years ago; I thought you'd want to see him."

"It's all right. I'm sure he won't stay long."

*****

Five minutes later, Samantha opened the door to the smiling face of Bobby Rooney. She had to admit he was even better looking than he'd been in high school. He had just a hint of gray at the temples. She imagined he'd have a full head of white hair by the time he was forty-five.

"Bobby, or should I call you Bob?"

"Most people know me as Bob, but you can call me anything you like. You look wonderful, Sammie. I didn't think you could be more beautiful than you were at sixteen, but I was wrong."

"I heard you were considering a political career, Bob. With that kind of flattery, you'll be very good at it," she laughed.

"I'm glad to hear you talked about me. I was afraid you'd forgotten about us now that you're getting married."

She wanted to tell him that she hadn't given him much thought in years and she'd forgotten about "us" long ago.

"Can I get you a glass of iced tea? Coffee? A drink?"

"Nothing, for now, I was hoping I could take you to dinner."

"That's nice, but no thank you, Bob. I'll be dining with my folks and soon to be in-laws this evening."

"I heard you were coming to town and I was hoping to get together with you to reminisce about the old days. I always thought we were meant to be together. Are you sure you want to marry this detective guy? I can offer you the life you deserve in the city."

"Are you out of your mind? After all these years, you think we could take up where we left off? We were kids back then. We talked about being together forever but forever didn't last long for one of us."

"I know I hurt you, but I want to make it up to you. You won't be sorry; I have the most beautiful penthouse apartment overlooking the city. I know many prominent people and my social life is full. I want to share that with you, Sam."

"Are you saying you need a wife to make you look like a better political candidate? The little woman who hangs on your every word?"

"Of course, that's part of it, but I thought of you when my manager told me it would be better if I married."

"And, what would I do with my fiancé? Dump him to run off to New York with you?"

"That sounds terribly harsh; you could let him down easy."

"I have no intention of letting him down at all. Not that it would mean anything to you, but I happen to love that detective guy. You can take your New York apartment, your snooty friends, and your social life and... well, never mind what you can do with it. Now, get out of here. I won't wish you luck in your run for congress because we don't need your type running the country."

Colleen heard the door slam behind Bobby Rooney and shouted, "Good for you, Samantha. I never really liked that boy; your father thought he was arrogant even back then."

"Can you believe the gall? Thank heaven he was out of my life years ago. Now, I'll grab that Nancy Drew book and forget about that absurd man."

CHAPTER 5

"Thank you for bringing me home, Samantha. I could have taken a cab," said Patsy, the following morning after she was discharged from the hospital.

"Don't be silly; it's no problem at all. I wanted to talk to you about those letters and the accident anyway. Has Allison been back to question you again?"

"She called just before you arrived at the hospital. The nurse told her I was being discharged and she should see me at home. I haven't heard from her, but suspect she'll be here shortly."

*****

As predicted, Officer Jennings arrived within five minutes.

"Ms. Burke," she said in her official voice, "our mechanics examined the brakes of your vehicle. They have determined there was some manipulation of the brake lines; however, the evidence is not conclusive enough to call for further investigation. I must say, I find it curious that, if the lines were cut, the cuts were not enough to cause your brakes to fail and result in bodily harm to you. And Old Gus identified you as the person who paid him to return your purse to the newspaper office. Those are two reasons that I'm suspicious of you and your motives. As far as I can tell, you haven't committed a crime. I'd suggest you stop trying to cause turmoil in this town by bringing up old accidental deaths."

"Believe me, ma'am, I don't wish to cause turmoil if it's all the same to you. I'd like to forget the whole thing."

Officer Jennings nodded to the two women and left Patsy's apartment without further conversation.

Samantha wondered what had happened in Allison's life to make her change so drastically. Allison had been the clown of the group; she always talked about wanting to be an actor. She was a member of the drama club and had a beautiful singing voice.

"Allison just isn't the same person as she was back in high school. I'm finding out how many changes there have been in my old friends."

"Allison is having problems with her daughter, Bella," said Patsy. "That girl is a handful."

"How could I have forgotten? Mom told me she adopted a child of a friend who died a few years ago."

"Yes, it's a very sad story; the girl was only five-years-old when her mother was diagnosed with breast cancer. Her husband couldn't deal with his wife's illness and took off. Poor little Bella was left in the care of her grandmother who was busy caring for her ill daughter. After Bella's mother died, Allison offered to take the girl in and she officially adopted her. Bella has had problems recently; she's ten-years-old now and rebellious. The last I heard, the child ran away and was gone overnight. 'Dear Patsy' would recommend counseling if only she were asked."

"You know something you're not saying, I can tell."

"You're a good detective, aren't you, Samantha? It's only speculation on my part. Do you remember my saying I observed more than you girls probably knew about each other?"

"Yes, I remember; what do you know that we didn't?"

"Do you remember when Allison put on a few extra pounds back at the end of the sophomore year?"

"Yes, I remember we were all on a health kick and got after her for cheating on her diet. You aren't saying...?"

"That's exactly what I'm saying. Didn't you notice her face filled out and she had no waistline? That summer she went to visit her aunt in California."

"She was gone until school started again. Are you saying she had a baby?" asked Samantha. "Why would she keep that a secret from us? She wasn't the only girl in our class to get pregnant."

"I don't think it was her idea," replied Patsy. "From what I hear, her father would have thrown her out of the house, and her mother insisted she hide her condition from everyone."

"Where did you get this information? It's hard to keep something like that secret, especially in a small town."

"Being a small town makes it easy to get people to talk. Nobody tells the whole story, but adding up bits and pieces helps to reach a conclusion that makes sense. Also, if you saw her, you'd see immediately that Bella Jennings is the perfect likeness to C.J. Sinclair."

"Oh, come on, you can't be serious," said Samantha.

"Oh, I'm serious all right," replied Patsy. "You see, Allison didn't go to California at all; she went to Evandale, gave birth to her baby and then gave the child to a couple in an open adoption. When it was clear that Bella would be alone after her adopted mother's death, Allison claimed she was a close friend and adopted the her own child back. So, six years after giving birth to her daughter, she was able to officially claim her as her own."

"Allison's father died when we were still in high school if I remember," said Samantha. "Why did she feel the need to keep silent?"

"That's a good question. To my knowledge, she hasn't told the truth even now; she'd benefit from counseling too. You have a strange look on your face, Samantha. What are you thinking?"

"You have me starting to believe C.J.'s death wasn't an accident after all. Is it possible Mr. Jennings found out about Allison's pregnancy and took matters into his own hands? He was a big man, as I remember; he could easily have overtaken C.J. on the cliff."

"There's another suspect we can add to the list. I hadn't thought about that possibility before."

"*Another* suspect? Who else is on your list?"

"Jody Logan and Erin Shaw were not on speaking terms because of C.J. It could have been either one of them. He was on a cliff; after all; it wouldn't take much to cause him to lose his footing." Patsy thought for a moment and then continued, "C.J.'s death gave Nick Turner the opportunity to become the star quarterback on the football team. Bobby Rooney never liked C.J.; he always thought you two had the hots for one another. I suppose half the school could have been jealous of him."

"You didn't mention me. Maybe I had a secret passion for my old pal."

"No, all your passion was for that loser, Bobby Rooney. I hope your new guy isn't anything like him."

"They are nothing alike," Samantha assured her. She told Patsy about the conversation she'd with Bobby the day before.

"I can see him as a politician; he's always been a smooth operator."

*****

"Samantha, have you seen the shrine they put up in the high school for C.J. a few years ago?"

"I heard about it. He was a hero, and his death only made him more so. Did his old teammates have something to do with it?"

"His teammates and everyone else in town. Nick Turner collected money and had a statue made in C.J.'s likeness. I haven't seen it, but I suspect there's a halo around his head."

"I'd like to see it; maybe I'll stop by the school and see if they'll let me check it out."

"I'll go with you; I can use my press pass. Believe it or not, they give 'Dear Patsy' one of those. If you don't mind, you can drop me off at the car rental. I feel lost without wheels."

"Shouldn't you be resting? You just got out of the hospital."

"I've rested enough. Shall we go?"

CHAPTER 6

Samantha hadn't been back to her old alma mater since graduation day. It looked smaller than she remembered. Memories came flooding back to her as she drove up the winding road. The building hadn't changed much except the ivy that always grew on the walls seemed to now envelope the entire façade. Summer classes were in full swing which meant fewer students roaming the halls than during the regular school year.

Mrs. Winthrop, the school secretary, recognized Samantha when she and Patsy walked into the front office.

"Samantha Degan, I was hoping I'd get a chance to see you." The woman eagerly reached into her desk and pulled out a copy of *Memoirs of Professor Stonehill*. "I hope you'll sign my book. I've told all my relatives scattered around the country that a famous author was one of my students."

Samantha didn't remember Mrs. Winthrop teaching a class, but there wasn't any harm in her claiming the students as her own.

"I'm not sure how famous I am, Mrs. Winthrop, but I will be happy to sign your book."

*****

After the three women chatted for several minutes, Patsy asked about seeing the display honoring C.J. Sinclair. Although she thought of it as a shrine, the school called it a display.

"Oh, yes, we're very proud of our display. C.J. Sinclair is sorely missed to this day. The young man had such promise and his life ended much too soon."

The older woman reached for a tissue and dabbed her moist eyes.

"We keep the doors locked during the summer. However, I do believe Coach Hartman is in his office. I'll call to see if he's available to unlock the doors."

Coach Ryan Hartman was deep into planning practice plays and welcomed the distraction. He walked into the office and held out his hand.

"Hello, I'm Ryan Hartman, I'll be happy to show you the sports department and all the displays, including the one honoring C.J. Sinclair. Did you know C.J.?" he asked.

Patsy had a difficult time catching her breath. She'd heard Amber talk about Coach Hartman but never expected him to be so handsome.

"Hello, Coach Hartman, I'm Samantha Degan and my friend here is Patsy Burke. We were classmates of C.J. It's nice of you to give us a tour."

"Please call me Ryan."

He led the way down the long corridor. Patsy tried to compose herself during the walk. What was wrong with her? She was a grown woman, and this man took her breath away. Samantha was enjoying the scene and noticed Coach Ryan Hartman's eyes were on Patsy too.

*****

Samantha gasped when she saw the life-size statue of C.J. "It's almost as if he's standing there, it looks just like him."

"I'm sorry, Samantha; I didn't consider how painful this would be for you. I shouldn't have suggested we come here today."

"No, I'll be fine; it's just a bit of a shock. You see, Ryan, C.J. and I lived next door to each other; we played together as children. We weren't as close in our high school days, but he was still like a brother to me."

"I'm sorry for your loss, Samantha. Let's go to my office. I just made a pot of coffee and I could use some help drinking it. I tell my guys not to drink caffeine but I don't always practice what I preach."

Patsy was finally able to speak coherently, "Ryan, how long have you been coaching at Ashville High?"

"Not long at all; this is my first coaching job. My dreams of having an NFL career died when I broke my arm during a practice skirmish. I was on the practice squad and couldn't be of much use to the team after that, so they cut me."

"That's too bad. So you took the coaching job because that was all that was left to you?" asked Patsy.

"To tell the truth, I wasn't good enough to play professionally. I coached Pop Warner in my off time and found coaching was something I liked doing. Coach Beardsley has a reputation for being one of the top high school coaches in the state, and I'm glad for the opportunity to learn from him. Are you a reporter? You have a knack for getting someone to open up about themselves."

"My field of study was journalism, but I haven't done much with it. I write an advice column in the local paper."

"'Dear Patsy'?"

"Yes, that's it; don't tell me you read advice to the lovelorn?"

"I started to after Mrs. Winthrop kept quoting you. You're funnier than the *Peanuts* comic strip. What does 'Mr. Dear Patsy' think of your column?"

"There is no 'Mr. Dear Patsy' anymore, he and I divorced before 'Dear Patsy' came into being. He was a sports hack and there wasn't room in his day for a wife."

"There wasn't room in my marriage for me when my ex discovered she hadn't married a football hero after all."

"I'm sorry, Samantha; we're ignoring you," said Ryan.

"Don't worry about me," she laughed. "I'm enjoying the conversation."

"It's close to lunchtime. Let me take you both to lunch," suggested Ryan.

"That sounds wonderful, but I really should get home; I'm supposed to be planning a wedding. Why don't you and Patsy go to lunch and I'll see you later."

She rushed out before Patsy could think of a good reason to stop her.

Fletch can't call me a matchmaker in this case. It's obvious they're perfect for each other and they aren't going to fight it. She had a smile on her face all the way to her car.

CHAPTER 7

Colleen Degan and Sandy Fletcher were busy tying lavender ribbons around mini champagne bottles adorned with photos of the bride and groom. Samantha resisted the temptation to remind the mothers that she and Fletch wanted a simple wedding. The wedding favors had already been purchased and Samantha couldn't deny they were a nice addition.

"Samantha, dear, you look happy. Are you enjoying being with your old friends?"

"To be honest, I'm enjoying my new friend, Patsy Burke. Mom, what do you know about Allison Jennings?"

"Not much anymore. Her mother never joined in any of the activities you girls were involved in when you were in school. I've heard her husband wouldn't allow her to have a social life. If I remember correctly, Allison wasn't permitted to do many of the things the other girls did."

"Her father wouldn't let her try out for cheerleader because the outfits were too skimpy and they weren't skimpy at all. Some of the girls were less covered up on a normal school day. Do you remember the summer Allison went to visit an aunt in California?" Samantha asked.

"Yes, you were envious of her spending the summer in California. I was a little envious of a vacation like that myself."

"Apparently, the trip wasn't anything to envy after all. According to Patsy, Allison was not in California.

The aunt she was visiting lived in Evandale and that's where she gave birth to her child."

"Is the child Bella?" Colleen asked.

"Why do you say that? Do you know something about Allison?"

"No, I don't know anything, and I probably shouldn't mention it, but I always questioned the adoption story. Allison was supposedly friends with Bella's mother. As far as I know, except for that summer, Allison rarely left Ashville for more than a weekend. She attended the community college and then entered the police academy here in town. I don't know when she'd have met this woman and become such great friends that she would adopt her child."

"Have you seen Bella, Mom?"

"I have, and I know what you're going to ask me. Yes, I do believe Bella is C.J.'s daughter. Not so much now, but when she first arrived in town, she looked exactly like him at that age. I don't know if anyone else could see the resemblance, but I remember C.J. very well. You two played together all the time; he was like one of the family."

"Mom, why didn't you ever mention this to me?"

"I guess I didn't think about it when you were in town. If Allison wanted the truth to be known, surely, she'd have told her best friends. The old man was dead by the time she brought Bella home, and didn't present any problems for her mother anymore."

"Has that grapevine of yours ever suggested C.J.'s fall might not have been accidental after all?"

"What are you saying? Do you think someone killed him? Oh, Samantha, after what happened to you in Lancashire, I wish you wouldn't get involved in these mysteries."

"I'm perfectly fine, Mom; there's no need to worry. I'm here to marry my best friend and not to stir up trouble. I'm beginning to wonder how I could have been so fooled by my old friend C.J. He wasn't a very nice guy, was he?"

*****

The sun beamed through the window of O'Leary's Irish Pub while Patsy and Ryan Hartman were enjoying their corned beef on rye, and each other's company.

"Are you planning to stay in Ashville for a while, or are you looking for greener pastures?" Patsy asked.

"By greener, do you mean more money?" he laughed. "I tried planning my future at one time, and it didn't work out too well for me. At this point, I'm satisfied being an assistant coach and learning what I can from Coach Beardsley. Coach is still a young man and I can't see him retiring anytime soon. Eventually, I'll be moving on."

"Are you setting your sights on a coaching job with the NFL?"

"That is a dream, but those jobs are few. There's pressure to win games at the high school level, but it doesn't compare to the professional level. Not only that, I'd like to plant roots in a town like Ashville. Maybe I'm just looking to avoid the competition out in the big world."

"I know how you feel, Ryan. If someone had told me five years ago I'd be writing an advice to the lovelorn column, I'd have laughed. I pictured myself living in New York and seeing my byline on breaking news stories. I probably shouldn't be so complacent, but I love the simple life of a small town. I didn't always love it here. I was the model for a high school wallflower and I can't blame anyone but myself for that label. I enjoyed wallowing in self-pity and had no reason to change."

"I can't believe that you were a wallflower, Patsy. I'd have guessed you were Miss Popularity in high school. If it hadn't been for football, I might have been the class nerd. I've had an interest in science for as long as I can remember. Along with my coaching duties, I'm a science teacher. It's the best of both worlds. Now, tell me why you're interested in C.J. Sinclair."

Patsy told him about the missing letters and the brakes that failed on her car.

"Maybe it's a coincidence. Allison Jennings, the investigating officer, seems to think I staged the whole thing but she can't prove it."

"What possible reason could you have for faking an accident that could have taken your life?"

"She seems to think I'm calling attention to a nine-year-old accident hoping to make trouble. If that was the case, I'd have thought of a better way than destroying my car in the process."

"What are your instincts telling you, Patsy?"

"That there's more to the story and that someone is afraid to talk about what they know."

"Just being in Ashville a few months, I know C.J. is still a local hero. The townspeople speak of him in hushed tones, like a saint."

"He was far from a saint. It wasn't totally his fault though; girls used to throw themselves at him. He was a popular guy and he made the most of it. He was not only the best quarterback Ashville High had ever known, he excelled in his studies, and was very handsome to boot."

"It sounds like you had a crush on him," Ryan said, fighting a pang of jealousy.

"No, he was so far out of my league, I didn't even fantasize about him," she laughed.

*****

"I came by to help with the wedding," said Samantha. "I've been here almost three days and have let you and Sandy do all the work."

"We have everything under control, dear. You should be visiting your friends while you're here. I know how happy everyone is to see you."

"I stopped by the police station and Allison has the day off. Maybe I'll drop by her house. Jody said she's still living with her mother."

"Yes, but don't expect to see Mrs. Jennings. The poor woman has become a recluse and hides in her bedroom most of the day."

"No wonder Allison is an unhappy person and her daughter runs away. It can't be very pleasant living there."

*****

Samantha knew the considerate thing to do would be to call her friend to announce her visit, but she wondered if Allison would agree to see her.

She rang the doorbell and could hear a television somewhere in the house. She saw the curtains move slightly and knew someone was watching her from the window.

"Mrs. Jennings," she called out, "it's Samantha Degan, an old friend of Allison's. I stopped by to say hello."

"Sorry, Samantha, it takes time for Mother to shuffle to her bedroom. She has to hide before I'm allowed to open a door," she said loud enough for her mother to hear. "What are you doing here? Defending your new best friend, Patsy Burke?"

"Allison, why would you say that? I came by to catch up with you, that's all. Are you going to invite me in or let me stand out here on the porch?"

"No, don't come in; let's go to the coffee shop on Main. I need to get out of here for a while."

Allison grabbed her purse and shouted—not too pleasantly—that she was going out and would be back before Bella got home from school.

*****

The coffee shop was nearly deserted in the early afternoon. They sat at a quiet table away from the counter and the few men who were finishing their coffee.

"Samantha, I'm glad you stopped by today. I'm sorry for the way I acted. Sometimes Mother is more than I can handle. She was in one of her moods this morning and I had to get out of there."

"Why do you stay in that house, if you don't mind me asking? Surely, the force pays enough for an apartment for you and Bella."

"It's not a matter of money. Mother is there with Bella when I'm working. For some reason, the two of them share a bond and it's a bond I'm not a part of. Bella can be a bit of a challenge. You've never met my daughter, have you?"

"I'm afraid not; I never spent more than a day or two in Ashville since high school. Studying and part-time jobs always cut into my time here. I'm glad I took this time to get reacquainted with my old friends. When can I meet Bella?"

"Anytime you can fit us into your busy schedule," Allison said sharply.

"Allison, what's wrong? Why are you so angry with me? I'm sorry I have been an absentee friend; maybe I should have made more of an effort to keep in touch these past few years."

"It's not you; it's me. I live with a woman who hasn't left the house in five years and a daughter who hates me. My mother cries for hours about missing my father and we both know what a bastard he was. My ten-year-old daughter is a female version of Damian and she isn't even a teenager yet. The good old boys at the station treat me like a piranha. Patsy Burke wants me to investigate C.J. Sinclair's death as a murder. To top it off, you strut into town with your perfect face, your perfect life, and your perfect guy. It's just not fair."

"Allison, my life is far from perfect but it's obvious you're troubled. Why don't you tell me about Bella and what you know of her life before you adopted her?"

"Bella's parents, Rich and Trudy Mason, were neighbors of my Aunt Celia in Evandale. I didn't see her often, but I could tell she was a happy baby. Trudy and Rich were good parents. Rich was a little standoffish but Trudy loved the little girl. Trudy was diagnosed with breast cancer when Bella was only four-years-old. Rich showed his true colors and left shortly after Trudy became ill.

"Bella didn't know where her father had disappeared to and didn't know how to cope with her mother's illness. Her grandmother, who took care of Trudy until the end, was so distraught by her daughter's death; she was in no position to care for a little girl. Bella didn't have anyone. I know it surprised a lot of people when I adopted her, but I couldn't let her go into foster care. You understand, don't you, Samantha?"

"I understand, you did what a mother would do."

"You know, don't you?"

"I don't know anything, but I'm guessing Bella is your child and she was born that summer when you told us you were in California."

"Obviously, I never did go to California. It was so hard not telling you girls the truth. I was afraid my father would not only kill me but kill my mother too. Believe me, the man was capable of murder."

"Why do you say that? Do you suspect him of murdering Bella's father?"

"You really are a detective, aren't you? How long have you known about C.J.?"

"Mom mentioned the resemblance today. Before that, I had no idea what you'd gone through at such a young age. We were all so consumed with our own lives, we didn't catch on to what you were going through."

"I hid my pregnancy well. You girls got on me about putting on weight. I tried to overeat when I was with you, and then would go home and throw up. I had morning, afternoon and evening sickness for the first six months."

"Did you tell C.J. he was going to be a father?"

"I did and he didn't believe me; he said I was trying to trap him with someone else's kid. He walked away from me that day and we never spoke again."

"What about Bella's adoptive father? Doesn't he still have parental rights?"

"I hired a private detective who was able to track him down. He readily relinquished his rights. I don't think he ever wanted Bella in his life in the first place."

Samantha's heart broke for Allison and Bella and for C.J. *What had happened to the boy she loved like a brother? When had he become so callous? He had so much going for him and it all went to his head. His mother died not knowing she was a grandmother. Frances Sinclair was a loving woman and would have welcomed C.J.'s child with open arms.*

"Allison, do you think Bella has a right to know the truth?"

"I plan to tell her when she's older. I'm afraid of what she might do if she finds out the truth in her fragile state."

"Have you considered family counseling?"

"Yes, I've thought of it, and I know I should be getting help for my girl. Her behavior started changing about six months ago. Before that, she was beginning to blossom into the sweet Bella she was before Trudy's illness. Samantha, I can't tell you how much better I feel just talking to you. I feel like a burden has been lifted off my shoulders now that you know the truth. I'm going to call for an appointment with a counselor as soon as I get home."

Allison's cell phone rang. She recognized the number of Bella's school. Allison's face turned scarlet. She thanked the caller and hung up.

"Bella's taking some extra credit classes in summer school. She asked to use the restroom and didn't return to class. One of the other students saw her riding her bike past the classroom window. Do you mind driving me home to see if she's there?"

"Of course, let's go."

Samantha left money on the table and they walked out of the restaurant. On the way to the car, Allison looked up and saw Bella riding down the middle of the street on her bike.

"Bella!" Allison shouted.

Bella saw her and attempted to turn the bike around, running into the curb in front of Krause Book Shop. Her body went over the handlebars and she landed on her head on the sidewalk.

Allison screamed and ran to her daughter. Mr. Krause came out of his store and fell to his knees beside Bella's motionless body. Samantha dialed 9-1-1, praying it wasn't too late.

CHAPTER 8

Allison rode in the ambulance with Bella, holding her limp hand as the paramedics continued to check her. She had seen many accident victims during her time as a police officer and knew how serious a head injury could be.

*****

After what seemed an eternity, the ambulance pulled into the emergency room entrance. Bella was taken to a cubicle where hospital staff were waiting. Allison stepped aside, never taking her eyes off her daughter.

*****

Samantha arrived shortly after, followed by Mr. Krause.

"Mr. Krause, I'm happy to see you. I don't know if you remember me."

"Oh, but I do remember you, Samantha. You were a favorite bookworm of Mrs. Krause. My Helga would be so proud that you are a writer yourself now."

Helga Krause had died several years ago. She and Frederick had opened the Krause Book Shop in the early sixties. They focused more on the pleasure of reading than the selling of books. Mrs. Krause captivated the children when she read stories to them. Her thick German accent added to their enjoyment. Samantha often dropped by the shop on her way home from school. The Krauses kept a corner of the store open with a supply of books for children of all ages.

"Mrs. Krause's appreciation of good storytelling is one of the reasons I began to write."

"Bella never met my Helga, but she has the same interest in reading as you had when you were her age. She stops by the shop almost every day after school. I was surprised when I saw her so early today. I was looking out the window when she took that terrible fall. She's such a special little girl; I wanted to come here to make sure she was all right."

"Allison is with her now," said Samantha. "I hope she comes out soon with news of Bella's condition. Head injuries are frightening."

"I wonder if Allison's mother knows about the accident," suggested Mr. Krause. "As soon as we hear something, I'll drive over there."

"It might not do much good; Allison says she won't open the door to anyone when she's alone in the house."

"I visit her quite often; Martha Jennings and my Helga were close. Helga made me promise I would take care of her friend after she died. I have kept that promise, although it isn't always easy. That husband of hers still has a hold over her even after his death. She does, however, allow me to sit at the kitchen table with her while we have afternoon tea."

"That's good to hear; I don't think Allison is aware of your visits," said Samantha.

"I don't think she is. Martha is a very private person; we talk mostly about books we've read. Helga knew some of her secrets but never revealed them to me. I get the feeling her husband was involved in something sinister. Maybe I'm letting my imagination get the better of me."

Samantha wondered if the *something sinister* involved C.J.'s accident. If Mr. Jennings had been responsible for the fall, what good would it do now? He could no longer be punished, and revealing it would only hurt his family.

*****

Allison walked through the doorway with a look of relief on her face.

"Bella is awake; they've taken her for a CT scan. The doctor thinks it's a concussion. She told me not to yell at her because she wasn't wearing her helmet. I told her we'd talk about that, and why she ditched school when she feels better. She seemed like her old self again.

"Mr. Krause, how nice of you to be here. Bella is so fond of you; she'll be glad to see you."

"I'm happy she will recover. I must leave to run an errand but I will be back shortly."

Samantha put her arm around her friend and guided her to a chair. Allison's heart stopped racing and Samantha noticed her color was returning to her cheeks.

"Wasn't it nice of Mr. Krause to leave his shop to check on Bella?" Allison said in almost disbelief.

"You have more friends in this town than you realize, Allison."

The outside doors to the waiting room opened and many of her fellow officers walked through.

"What's happened?" she asked the captain. With this many officers in one location, she feared the hospital was in danger.

Captain Riley smiled at her. "We're here for you, Officer Jennings. The minute your daughter's accident was called into the station, we rounded up every available officer. We're here to stand by a fellow officer in trouble."

Allison was touched and tried her best to hold her head high and fight the urge to cry.

One by one, each of the men approached her with words of comfort. For the first time since she'd joined the force, Allison felt she belonged and was part of a team. She told them Bella was going to be fine and thanked them for their offers to help.

Captain Riley said to take as much time as she needed to be with Bella through her recovery.

One by one, her fellow officers saluted her as they walked to the door. When the last man left the building, Allison turned to Samantha and burst into tears.

*****

Doctor Remington approached and told Allison that the CT scan showed no signs of permanent damage. He thought it best, however, for Bella to stay overnight for observation.

Samantha offered to drive Allison home to pack a change of clothing for herself and Bella, "or I could bring the clothes to you, that is, if you trust me to pick out an outfit for you."

"I trust you. In the old days, you always supervised my wardrobe. I don't think I ever went to Melbourne's Department store without you and Jody and Erin."

Samantha laughed, thinking of the times they'd wear each other's clothes. They had traded so often, she would lose track of what belonged to her and what belonged to the others. There were so many happy memories until the day C.J. died. Samantha still felt a tinge of pain when she thought about the tragedy.

"On second thought, Samantha, it will freak Mother out if you're in the house without me. I'll call Decker later; he can drive me to the house and I'll get my car too."

"Do I sense something in the air with Officer Decker? He is a cutie."

"Decker? No, he is a hunk though, isn't he? He's a rookie who always treated me like his maiden aunt. Not only that, he's taken. He's engaged to a sweet little thing who can't be more than nineteen. I'm sure you'd like to see all your old friends married off, but there isn't one single guy on the entire force."

"Bummer! I'm going to leave you to be with your daughter. If you need anything at all, please call me."

*****

Allison watched Bella as she slept peacefully for about an hour. She was dozing off herself when she heard Bella's voice.

"Mom, are you mad at me?"

"Oh, Bella, I'm not mad. I'm so happy you're going to be all right. I couldn't bear it if I lost you."

"You don't mean that," Bella whispered. She looked up and her face lit up, "Grandma, you're here!"

Allison turned to see her mother standing there looking like a scared rabbit. She was holding Mr. Krause's arm so tightly that Allison worried she was cutting off his circulation.

"Mother, I can't believe my eyes. Mr. Krause, how did you get her out of the house?"

"I told her Bella was hurt and she wanted to see her," he said, smiling.

"Mother, come sit next to Bella. You can see she's looking good; she even has some color in her cheeks." Allison stood up to let her mother take her seat.

"Mr. Krause, how did you get my mother to leave the house? She hasn't seen the light of day for over five years now."

"We've made some slow progress. My Helga and your mama were good friends before Helga passed. She made me promise to encourage Martha to get out of the house occasionally. Until today, she's only been as far as the backyard."

He gently guided Mrs. Jennings to the chair next to Bella's bed.

"My beautiful Bella, I was so worried something terrible had happened to you," Martha Jennings said, her shaking hand grasping her granddaughter's fingers.

"I'm all right, Grandma. I bumped my head. I've never seen you any place but inside our house. You look different to me."

"Mr. Krause said you were hurt. I had to see you for myself. I'm ready to leave now, Frederick. please take me home."

Allison was afraid her mother was going to have a panic attack right there in the room. She walked toward the older woman, but Mr. Krause had his arm wrapped around her shoulder and was already calming her down.

"It's all right, Martha, you're safe here with Allison and Bella, I'm right by your side."

Martha sat quietly for another minute or so and then looked pleadingly into Frederick Krause's eyes. "May we leave now, Frederick?"

"Yes, Martha; we'll leave now. You've been very brave today. Tomorrow we'll walk around the block; you'll be able to see all the beautiful flowers we drove by on the way here."

Martha kissed Bella's hand and smiled at Allison. "I'm going home now," she said with relief.

"We'll see you tomorrow, Mother. I'll be staying with Bella tonight."

*****

After her grandmother left the room, Bella glared at her mother.

"I thought Grandma was afraid to leave the house. Did you lie about that too?"

"Bella, what are you talking about? You know Grandma hasn't been outside in years. I was as surprised to see her as you were. Why would you think I'd lie about that?"

"Because you lie about everything. You don't have to stay with me tonight; I know you'd rather be with your girlfriends."

"Bella, what has gotten into you? I want to be with you tonight. Why do you think I'm lying to you? Maybe that conk on the head made you cuckoo."

"You lied about my mom, Trudy, and you lied about adopting me."

"I don't understand what you're talking about, Bella," Allison said with the sinking feeling that she knew very well what Bella was saying.

"You were my mother when I was a baby, and you didn't want me so you gave me away. I heard you and Grandma talking, and you told her I should never have been born."

Bella began to sob. The crying made her head hurt and she cried even more.

"Oh, baby, that's not true. I always wanted you. I loved you even before you were born."

Bella fell asleep in Allison's arms. She needed the rest now but when she woke up, Allison would tell her the truth. She prayed she hadn't lost her daughter forever.

CHAPTER 9

Patsy Burke sat on her sofa reminiscing about her time with Ryan Hartman that afternoon. He had driven her to the car rental place in town and then they drove off in different directions.

She thought they'd clicked earlier, but he never asked for her phone number or talked about getting together again. *Oh, well,* she thought aloud, *I'm doing fine on my own; I have nobody to answer to or worry about. I have my work and a few friends to laugh with. Who needs a man?*

The doorbell rang, startling her, and abruptly ending her reverie. She opened the door to Ryan and smiled.

"I probably shouldn't just show up on your doorstep like this, but I was driving by and thought I'd see how your car is running."

"You happened to be driving by?" she smiled. "How did you know where I lived?"

"Okay, you've got me. I saw your address when you were filling out the rental agreement. Did I tell you I have a photographic memory?"

"That's a nice trait to have, especially when you go to the grocery store and forget your list. Please come in, I'm having a glass of wine, would you like to join me?"

"Sure, it's no fun to drink alone. I take that back, I've had some of the best conversations with myself and a six pack on cold, lonely nights."

Patsy's house was cozy and furnished comfortably. The overstuffed sofa was her favorite place to sit and unwind after a busy day at work. The *Ashville Tribune* was a small-town paper with less staff than most. Along with the 'Dear Patsy' column, her job consisted of editing other columnists' work and re-writing some articles.

Patsy pulled two steaks out of the freezer that she was saving for a special occasion. She defrosted them in the microwave while Ryan fired up the grill on her patio. She sliced tomatoes and cucumbers to add to a package of ready-made salad and popped frozen corn on the cob into a pan of boiling water.

After dinner, they sipped more wine. Ryan was wondering how to maneuver her into the living room and onto the sofa. Patsy was about to ask if he'd like to go inside when they heard a crash.

They both jumped from their chairs and ran into the house. It was dusk but they could see the shattered window the minute they walked into the living room. A large rock had landed on the floor, just missing the television. Glass covered her beautiful sofa; she wondered if she'd ever be comfortable sitting on it again. Ryan ran out the front door but saw nothing. He came back inside and put his arm around Patsy to comfort her.

"We'll have to call the police, Patsy; this was definitely not an accident. There's a note wrapped around the rock, but we'd better not touch it."

Patsy walked over to the rock. "I can read it from here. It says GET OUT OF ASH.... The rest is hidden, but it doesn't take a genius to know it says, *Get out of Ashville.*"

*****

Officer Decker arrived in less than ten minutes.

"Ms. Burke, I don't think you could have staged this by yourself. I know Officer Jennings questioned your accident, but this should convince her someone is trying to harm you. Do you have any idea who it could be?"

"I know who; it's the person who killed C.J. Sinclair or someone who's protecting the murderer."

"I can write up a report to send to your insurance company," said Officer Decker. "That's about all I can do for you."

"That's all you can do?" cried Patsy. "Can't you take fingerprints or something?"

"We can do that, but I don't think we'll find any. It's a certainty that the rock was wiped clean before it was thrown through the window. We'll keep it and the note as evidence in case they try something else. In the meantime, you might want to keep a low profile."

"Thank you for your advice, Officer," Patsy grinned.

"You're welcome, although I know you won't take it."

*****

Patsy's neighbor, Jim Harding, came over when he saw the police car lights flashing. He was standing in the open doorway.

"Patsy, what's happened? Are you all right?"

"I'm fine, Jim, but my window isn't." She introduced him to Ryan.

"I don't suppose you have any plywood in your basement?" Ryan asked Patsy.

"If she doesn't, I do," said Jim. "I'll get it and some strong nails."

"You can't put nail holes in my window casings; I just painted them."

"After the window's replaced, I'll help you patch up the holes and repaint. You don't have a choice."

Patsy agreed, but didn't like it. She was more determined than ever to get to the bottom of the mystery now. Ryan insisted she pack a bag and come home with him. He told her he had a guest bedroom with a lock on the door. She agreed, but not because she was afraid to sleep in her own bed.

Ryan lived in a newer apartment building not too far from the high school. Patsy thought it looked like a real home and not a typical bachelor pad.

Ryan could tell she wasn't prepared for what she saw.

"Were you expecting to see a futon and lava lamp on an old TV table? Maybe beer bottles strewn around on the floor?"

"Not the beer bottles, but yes, you did surprise me. You have very good taste, Mr. Hartman."

"Thank you, Ms. Burke. I'm just your typical homebody. I'm either here or at school. You must be exhausted; let me show you the guest bedroom. You will be comfortable there."

Patsy was pleasantly surprised; the room was painted a soft blue. There was a queen-sized bed with a blue and gray billowy comforter on top. A small chest of drawers and a matching dressing table were on either side of the bed. The pictures were of lakes and mountains. It would be a comfortable room for either a man or a woman.

"This is lovely, Ryan. To be honest, I don't think I could sleep a wink. If you want to go to bed, feel free. I've brought along a novel I'm reading and I'll be fine. I won't make a peep."

"I'm not tired either. Would you like to watch some television? Maybe it will make both of us sleepy."

They sat on the sofa with the television on. Ryan turned the sound low, but it didn't matter, they weren't paying any attention to the show.

"Would you like to talk about what happened tonight?" Ryan asked. "I understand if you'd rather not."

"I'm wondering who sent those letters in the first place. I'd guess they wanted someone to investigate C.J.'s death. Did they chicken out and decide to steal the letters back? How did they know the letters were in my purse and I was headed to the police station with them? They only meant to scare me when the brakes failed in my car. The rock tonight was another scare tactic. They haven't scared me; they've just made me more determined to find answers."

CHAPTER 10

The sun beamed through the sheer curtains in Samantha's bedroom, disturbing the dream taking place in her mind. She walked down a long path in the park holding her father's arm, Fletch waited by the pond for her, his arms opened wide. She buried her head in the pillow, trying to recapture that wonderful dream. It didn't work. She was awake and there was no going back to sleep. She and Fletch had only been apart for a few days, but she ached for the feel of his arms around her.

Right on cue, her cell phone rang. She knew it was Fletch by the ring tone.

"Good morning, husband-to-be. I just woke up from the most wonderful dream about you."

"I'm glad you're awake. I waited as long as I could to call you. I miss you, Samantha; I don't think I can wait until the end of the week to see you. Would you mind if I drove to Ashville tomorrow?"

"Would I mind? I'd love it. Are you sure you can't come today?"

"I'd better not push it with the captain; he isn't too keen on letting me leave early. Luckily, there isn't much criminal activity in Lancashire this week."

*****

Colleen noticed the smile on her daughter's face when she came downstairs for breakfast.

"Why do I think you've spoken with Fletch already this morning?" she said. "I'd say you're in love with the guy."

"You'd be right, Mom. He's driving to Ashville tomorrow. I can't wait to see him again."

*****

Looking at her watch, Samantha thought it wasn't too early to call Patsy. She was wondering how lunch with Ryan Hartman had gone the day before.

"Hi, Patsy. I'm calling for the low-down on Ryan. Did you have a good time yesterday?"

"Yes, we did. In fact, I'm sitting across from him at the breakfast table in his apartment."

"Wow, you two didn't waste any time. I could tell the sparks were flying when I saw you together yesterday. I won't keep you, but I want to hear all about it. Call me later."

"It's not what you think," Patsy laughed. "Mr. Hartman was a perfect gentleman, darn it." She winked at Ryan. "We did have a nice lunch and dinner too. Unfortunately, our evening was cut short by the jerk who hurled a rock through my window."

"Patsy, are you all right? That's terrible; someone wants you to drop the C.J. matter."

"I'm fine, but I can't say as much for my window. Ryan and my neighbor, Jim, will be replacing it today. There was a note wrapped around the rock telling me to, *Get out of Ashville.*"

"If this was the first instance of violence against you, I'd say it was a childish prank. That reminds me; your theory about Allison and Bella Jennings is correct. Allison told me the story yesterday. I was with her when Bella fell off her bike and ended up with a concussion. Allison is going to come clean to everyone that she's Bella's birth mother. You were also right about C.J. being the child's father. I'm wondering about Mr. Jennings. If he found out about the pregnancy, I don't doubt he'd have gone after C.J. He had a mean streak in him."

"It's obvious Allison doesn't want me to dig into C.J.'s death. She might be hiding her father's involvement, or maybe her own."

"The doctor admitted Bella for observation last night. I know Allison arranged to spend the night with her. I can't believe she left the hospital to toss a rock through your window. I'm going to talk to Jody and Erin today. They have a strained relationship and I want to know if there's more to it than their shared feelings for C.J. Enjoy your breakfast with Ryan; I'll talk to you later if I find out anything interesting."

*****

Erin Shaw had received her broker's license and had opened her own real estate company. Her schedule was flexible, so when Samantha called to ask her for coffee, she was happy to leave the office.

Samantha smiled when she saw her friend walk into the coffee shop in her stylish suit and three-inch heels.

"You look so professional, Erin. I feel like a frump in my capris and flip-flops."

"Believe me, I'd rather be dressed like you," Erin said as she kicked her heels off and slid them under the table. "I'm so glad you called, I wanted to talk to you one-on-one without Jody and Kate monopolizing the conversation."

"I'm sorry; I didn't realize they were doing that. I'm afraid I talked about myself a lot too. Tell me how's it going with you, Erin?"

"You were fine; it's those two. When we get together, Jody raves about her wonderful husband and her two bastard kids. I'm sorry, Samantha, I know I sound like a terrible person. The truth is, I'm jealous of both of them. They have husbands and I have no one. Did you know I dated Will Logan when he first came to town? I thought we had something special going until he met Jody. She batted those mascara-laden eyelashes at him and that was the end of us. He didn't care that she had two children by another man; he married her anyway. That's the second guy she's stolen from me."

"The first was C.J. Sinclair," said Samantha. "I don't know anything about Will, but from what I'm hearing about C.J., I don't think he was worthy of you."

"C.J. was wonderful; he was everything I've ever wanted. Even Will didn't measure up. C.J. was my first, you know. I was only sixteen when we first made love, but he made me feel like a woman."

"How did you find out he was with Jody too?" asked Samantha.

"They were standing outside English class when I came around the corner. I stopped when I recognized their voices. He was telling Jody how much he wanted to make love to her again; he said all the things he'd said to me many times before. Suddenly, his words sounded dirty and not loving at all. I hated him at that moment and I hated Jody even more. I ran down the hallway in the opposite direction, I went into the bathroom and threw up. I didn't speak to Jody for the rest of the day. When she asked me what was wrong, I told her. She was as surprised as I was that C.J. was seeing both of us. She and I didn't speak again until the day C.J. died. Our friendship is a lie. I still don't like her."

"Did C.J. know you and Jody found out about each other?"

"He knew and he enjoyed it. Even though I hated him, I still loved him and couldn't stop seeing him. I used to watch him when he hiked on the cliffs. I often thought how easy it would be to push him off the rocks. I couldn't believe it when I found out he'd fallen and wondered if I'd cursed him somehow."

"Do you think it's possible someone did push him, Erin?"

"I've often wondered if Jody did; she thought she loved him too."

"Does Jody know you were dating Will?" asked Samantha.

"Of course, she knew; that's the only reason she went after him. She was trying to get back at me for loving C.J. I don't think she really loves Will. She just needed a father for those boys."

Samantha worried about the bitterness she heard in her friend's voice. Erin had admitted she thought of pushing C.J. off the cliff. It gave her chills to think her friend could be a murderer.

Erin's assistant called, interrupting them. Something had gone wrong with a listing and she had to return to the office immediately. Erin left the coffee shop, wondering if she'd said too much to Samantha.

*****

Allison waited for Doctor Remington to arrive and discharge Bella. The nurse said he'd had an emergency and would be delayed for more than an hour. Bella was better, but scowling at her mother.

"Eat your breakfast, Bella, and then we'll talk about you and me."

Although Bella didn't want to obey her mother, she was hungry and the pancakes on the plate smelled too good to pass up. She ate every morsel and even finished the sliced peaches in a dish on her tray.

"Bella, I don't know what you heard when Grandma and I were talking, but I never once wished you hadn't been born.

"I was fifteen years old; I thought I loved a boy in my science class. He was handsome and smart and very popular. My father was very strict and didn't allow me to go to dances at school or any of the things teenagers liked to do. I was very shy around boys, but this boy made me feel comfortable. He asked me to go to the movies with him, but I had to turn him down because I knew my father would never let me go. Eventually, I began skipping out on the last class of the day to meet him. I knew what I was doing was wrong but it didn't stop me from giving in to him.

"I suspected I was pregnant and bought a test and took it while I was in school. I didn't take it at home because I was afraid of what my father would do if he found out. The test was positive. I was scared, but I knew I wanted the baby. I told the boy and he said he didn't believe me."

Allison let the information sink in before she continued. She told Bella about going away to give birth and that she wanted to keep her baby, but it was impossible because of her father. He wouldn't have let her come home if he'd known.

"Aunt Celia was a wonderful woman, but she couldn't take us in. That was when she introduced me to Trudy and Rich Mason. Trudy promised to take care of you and love you. She said I could see you when I came to visit Aunt Celia.

"When Trudy became ill and there was no hope that she would live, she asked me to adopt you. I was sorry Trudy died but I was happy to have you in my life again.

"I always intended to tell you the truth about your birth. I was waiting until you were older and could fully understand. I want you to know that I have always loved you. I didn't want to give you away, but I didn't think I had a choice. After my father died, I wanted to take you back, but by then, Trudy and Rich were the only parents you'd ever known. I couldn't just take you from them."

Bella sat quietly. Allison wished she would say something.

Finally, after a long silence, she asked, "Who's my father?"

"His name was C.J. Sinclair; he died several years ago," Allison answered.

"Awesome! My dad is C.J. Sinclair? There's a statue of him in the high school. Sweet! Wait until I tell Marcy Lundgren, she'll flip." Bella threw her arms around her mother. "I love you, Mom, and I'm glad you got me back."

"Did you understand everything I just told you?" asked Allison.

"Sure, we learned all about that stuff in school. I do know where babies come from, you know," an irritated Bella replied.

At that moment, Dr. Remington popped his head in the door.

"This is a happy twosome," he said. "Would a pretty young lady like to go home or are you having too much fun here?"

"I'd like to go home, Dr. Remington. I want to tell everyone my real father is C.J. Sinclair," Bella said with pride.

Dr. Remington gave Allison a questioning look and smiled before he left the room to sign the discharge papers.

*****

"Knock, knock," said Samantha. "I thought I'd stop by to see the patient, but it looks like she's ready to go home."

"Bella, this is an old friend of mine, Samantha Degan. She's the lady who's getting married this weekend. We'll be going to her wedding in the park."

"Hello, Miss Samantha. Do you know who my father is? He's C.J. Sinclair. Isn't that cool?"

"That's very cool," Samantha replied, looking in Allison's direction.

"Mom, can I say goodbye to the nurses?"

"Go ahead, but don't stay at the nurses' station for too long; we'll be leaving soon," said her mother.

"Sounds like you told Bella the story of her birth."

"I did and she seems to have accepted it without question. She's excited that C.J. is her father. I didn't know she knew about him. He has quite a reputation."

"This is probably none of my business, Allison, but do you think C.J.'s father should be told he has a granddaughter?"

"Didn't the Sinclairs move away after C.J. died?"

"Yes, they moved to South Carolina. Frances Sinclair passed away a few years ago. George remarried recently. My folks visited them last summer. The new Mrs. Sinclair has a bunch of kids and grandchildren. Mom says George is happier than he's been since before the accident."

"I can't just call the man and say, *Guess what? You have a granddaughter.* He probably wouldn't believe me, I don't have proof that C.J. is Bella's father."

"I suppose that would be awkward. I could ask Mom to call him. She mentioned Bella's resemblance to C.J. the other day."

"Does everyone in town know the secret I've tried to keep all these years?"

"I'm sure not everyone knows. C.J. was part of our lives for years; few people knew him as a kid like our family did. Why don't I give her a call?"

*****

Samantha walked out into the lobby to make the call to her mother. She didn't want to take a chance that Bella would overhear and face the possible rejection of George Sinclair.

Samantha remembered Mr. Sinclair as being a congenial man who was always kind to her and the other kids in the neighborhood. Her mother would be a better judge of whether he'd accept his granddaughter or not.

"Hi, Mom, your instincts about Bella Jennings were correct; she is C.J.'s daughter. Allison is willing to tell Mr. Sinclair about Bella; how do you think he'll take it?"

"He'll be thrilled; does Allison need his phone number?"

"Actually, Allison needs you to pave the way. She's afraid if she calls him unexpectedly, he won't believe her. Do you think you could talk to him first? Allison is willing to have a DNA test if he needs proof."

"Bella looks enough like a Sinclair that he won't question that C.J. is her father. I'll call him right away and get back to you."

"Thanks, Mom; I knew I could count on you."

CHAPTER 11

Colleen Degan's hands were shaking when she reached for her address book to search for George Sinclair's phone number.

"Colleen, are you all right?" asked her concerned husband, Archie Degan.

"I'm fine. Oh Archie, the most wonderful news! George Sinclair has a granddaughter. I suspected it was the case but now it's been confirmed. I'm going to call him right away."

"Hold on a minute, sweetheart. What's this all about? C.J. has been gone for years. Who's claiming to be his child?"

"You remember Allison Jennings? She was a friend of Samantha's. The poor girl got herself in trouble in high school. It's a long story but her daughter, Bella, is C.J.'s child. Oh, Archie, if you could see that little girl, you'd know it's true. She looks so much like her daddy."

"Colleen, this girl might be telling the truth, but she could be fabricating the story too. George Sinclair isn't exactly a pauper. I'd like to see some proof of the girl's parentage before you get George all worked up. He's never gotten over the loss of his son and I don't want to see anyone take advantage of his vulnerability."

"Archie, the girl is ten-years-old; I don't want George to miss any more years from her life than he already has. Allison has agreed to a DNA test; she wouldn't be willing to do that if she was trying to swindle George."

"Do what you feel you should. Jack and I have a tee time at Ashville Pines. We should be finished before one if you and Sandy would like to meet us at the club."

*****

Colleen picked up the phone to call her friend George. She hoped Archie was wrong; he didn't know Allison Jennings as well as she did. Not that she knew Allison as well as she knew Samantha's other friends. Allison was a pretty girl with a beautiful smile. Colleen suspected that years ago that she didn't have a happy home life. She'd often heard stories of the ill-natured Mr. Jennings. He'd caused his share of problems with shop owners in town. She didn't think many people shed a tear when he suffered a heart attack and died.

Colleen could hear ringing on the line indicating a connection. Her heart began to pound in her chest; *what will she say? What was the relationship between Allison and C.J.? Were they in love? Did C.J. know the girl was pregnant?*

"Hello."

It was too late; there was no going back now.

"Sharon, this is Colleen Degan; how are you?"

"Colleen, it's so good to hear your voice. George and I were talking about you and Archie just the other day. We hoped you were planning another trip down south. We had so much fun when you two visited us last summer."

"We should do that; Archie and I enjoyed that trip too. Sharon. I'm calling on another matter. Is George home?"

"No, he's at his Kiwanis meeting this morning. They usually go out for brunch after the meeting. I don't expect him for three or more hours. I hope nothing is wrong."

"No, nothing is wrong. Maybe I should tell you what I'm calling about. You can tell me how you think George will react."

"Of course; it sounds serious."

Colleen proceeded to tell her friend the reason for her call. She admitted she had no proof except the girl's resemblance to George's son. When she finished, there was silence on the other end.

"Sharon, are you still there?"

"Yes, I'm here. I'm sorry but I'm overwhelmed with joy for George. If there is even a remote possibility this girl is George's granddaughter, he'll be elated. Is there any way you can send us a picture of Bella?"

"I'm sure my daughter can work that out. I'll call her as soon as we hang up. Allison will, no doubt, have a recent photo of Bella she can e-mail to you."

*****

Samantha offered to drive Allison and Bella home from the hospital because Allison's car was still at her house. Bella was full of chatter on the short ride from the hospital. Allison was beaming at the change in her daughter.

"Bella, if I'd known you were going to be this happy, I'd have told you the truth long ago."

"Mom, you always told me it was better to tell the truth. You said if I did, you wouldn't be mad at me, no matter what I did wrong. I'm not mad at you anymore because you told me the truth and because C.J. Sinclair is my father."

"Bella, your father wasn't perfect; no one is. He was a teenage boy who was handsome, smart and a great athlete. The town has made a hero of him since he died but he did have his flaws too."

"Like knocking you up?"

"Bella, I don't want to hear you use that kind of language."

"Chill out, Mom. All the kids talk like that. Don't you ever watch TV? They say a lot worse than that on Grandma's shows."

Samantha laughed. "Two days ago, you were afraid Bella would never speak to you again."

"I know," said Allison. "I've created a monster."

*****

After making sure Allison and Bella were settled and didn't need anything at the store, Samantha left them on the couch watching an old Disney movie.

She drove by Jody Logan's house. Jody was in the front yard watering her flowers.

"Come in and have a cup of coffee with me. Will is fishing with the children. The house is so quiet without them, I could use a distraction."

They walked through the garage and into the mud room.

"I know it's silly of me, but do you mind taking your shoes off. I don't want to risk skid marks on my floor."

Samantha didn't mind and removed her tennis shoes. She was happy she'd worn socks without holes in the toes.

Jody led her into the kitchen—the room was spotless. The counter showed no signs of anyone living there. The cabinets were pure white and the appliances sparkled. Samantha couldn't believe this was the home of two young boys.

"Jody, when did you become a neat freak? Are you the same girl who never made her bed through high school?"

"Will likes a clean house, and I don't work. I have nothing to do all day but clean and cook. Not all of us are famous authors like you, Samantha."

"I didn't mean anything by it, Jody, and I'm not exactly famous."

"Have you talked to Erin since the other day when we were at your Mom's house?"

"Yes, I did see her."

"I suppose she talked about me. She hates me, you know. She thinks I ruined her life because C.J. loved me more than he loved her."

"I can't believe you two are still feuding over something that happened in high school."

"What she did was unforgivable, Samantha. C.J. broke it off with me because of her. He said I was stronger than Erin and he didn't want to hurt her. He didn't care that he hurt me."

"Jody, you and Erin are blaming each other for being hurt when it's C.J. you should be upset with. He was using you both, can't you see that?"

"You don't understand, Samantha. I loved him. I followed him to the cliffs after he told me he didn't want to see me anymore. He shoved me away. I thought I was going to fall, but he caught me and accused me of trying to get his attention by making it look like I was attempting suicide. I wanted to kill him."

"Did you, Jody?"

"Did I what?"

"Did you kill C.J.?"

"What are you saying? Do you think I could kill a person? I thought we were friends. What kind of a question is that?"

"I'm sorry, Jody, but you're the one who said you wanted to kill him. He's dead and there's a possibility it wasn't an accident like the town thinks."

"Before you accuse me, you should know I wasn't the only one who wanted him dead. How about your boyfriend, Bobby Rooney? Did you know Bobby started a fight with C.J. over you? C.J. got the better of him, though; Bobby had a shiner for a week."

"I remember when Bobby had a black eye. He said he ran into a door."

"Don't tell me you believed him?"

"I had no reason not to. Why would Bobby want to fight with C.J.?"

"Bobby was jealous of you and C.J. I swear he'd turn green when he saw the two of you together. No one in school thought you and C.J. were just friends."

"We were just friends; how many times have I told you he was like a brother to me? Maybe that's why I ignored his behavior. I still can't believe C.J. was such a sleaze. Shall we change the subject?"

"I suppose you want to talk about your perfect wedding to the perfect man?"

"Jody, why are you acting this way? What have I done to make you so hostile?"

"For one thing, you're hanging out with Patsy Burke. She's trying to cause trouble for us. I wish she'd get out of Ashville."

Those are the exact words that were on the note wrapped around the rock thrown at Patsy's window. Is it possible Jody was the one who threw it? "Jody, what are you worried about?"

"Never mind; I need to get back to work. Thanks for stopping by."

Samantha left her friend's house. *What had happened to everyone? When did her best friends become so defensive? Jody's behavior today bordered on psychopathic.* She couldn't wait until tomorrow when Fletch would be here to bring calmness back into her life.

CHAPTER 12

Sharon Sinclair waited nervously for her husband's return. She hadn't been able to take her eyes off the picture of Bella Jennings. There was no doubt in her mind that this beautiful little girl was George's granddaughter. She was the image of pictures she'd seen of C.J. She had Frances Sinclair's eyes too. Sharon never knew Frances; she'd met George after his wife's death. He had such sadness in his eyes the day they met at the Kiwanis fundraiser. Sharon had accompanied her friend, Joan, that Saturday afternoon. It was a beautiful day and the fundraiser was an excuse to be outside and help with a worthy cause too.

Sharon's husband had died unexpectedly two years before she met George. Sharon was just beginning to get back into the world of the living after Ed's death. She and Ed were college sweethearts; they were as much in love after thirty-five years of marriage as they had been the day they met. They'd celebrated the marriage of the last of their five children and were looking forward to being empty nesters.

Sharon never expected to find happiness with a man again. She and George Sinclair were both suffering from the loss of their spouses and found comfort in each other's company. Eventually, the friendship turned to love and they married with the blessing of Sharon's children.

*****

Sharon heard George's car pull into the garage of their comfortable townhouse. She greeted him at the door with a kiss as she always did when he returned to their home.

"You're nervous. Has something happened to one of the children?" George asked.

"No, it's not anything bad; I don't know where to begin."

"Sharon, just tell me. What you have to say can't be worth my having a nervous breakdown over waiting to hear what's on your mind."

"It's about C.J. There's a very real possibility he fathered a child when he was in high school."

"What are you talking about? Who told you this nonsense?" George asked.

"Colleen Degan called this morning. Did you know Allison Jennings from Ashville?"

"The name sounds familiar; I do remember a Jennings from there. He was a crude character. He had a wife and a daughter. The wife was a timid thing; Frances always said she was afraid of her own shadow."

"Allison is their daughter. She got pregnant at fifteen and her mother arranged for her to leave town before she gave birth to the baby. It's a long story but the child was adopted by a couple, ant then the woman died and Allison took the child back to Ashville when she was five or six-years-old. C.J. was little Bella's father."

The color drained from George's face when Sharon handed him her cell phone showing him the picture of Bella. He gazed at the photo in disbelief. "It can't be!"

Sharon watched as the tears welled in her husband's eyes. Had she made a mistake showing him the picture? She held her breath until he spoke again.

"Sharon, maybe I'm being a fool, but I believe this child is C.J.'s. I must see her for myself; I'm going to get the first flight out of here. He picked up his cell phone. Will you come with me?"

"Of course, I will," Sharon said while praying that George's heart wouldn't be broken if Bella wasn't his granddaughter.

*****

Samantha drove by Patsy Burke's house on her way back to her childhood home. She stopped when she saw Ryan and another man lifting a glass window into place in the front of the house.

Patsy was inside doing her best to remove the shards of glass that seemed to have embedded themselves into the carpet. She glanced toward the window and saw Samantha's VW slow down at the curb.

"Samantha, come in." She introduced her visitor to her neighbor, Jim.

"The window looks as good as new, Patsy."

"I wish I could say the same for the carpet. Jim has a power vacuum he's going to bring over when the guys are through with the window. I'm not going to walk around barefoot for a while."

"Do the police have a clue about who did this? It's such a childish thing to do."

"They consider it random mischief. I've checked with all the neighbors and no one saw anything suspicious last night. It's not all bad. Ryan insists on staying with me tonight. I've never had someone so concerned with my safety before."

"He seems like a great guy; I'm happy for you."

"What have you been up to today, Samantha?"

"It's been a busy day. Allison told Bella the truth. It seems she overheard her mother and grandmother talking and misunderstood the conversation. That is the reason she's been acting out. After Allison told her that C.J. Sinclair was her father, all was forgiven. Even in death, C.J. is charming women of all ages.

"My mother was going to call George Sinclair this afternoon to tell him he has a granddaughter, I haven't talked to her to find out his reaction."

"Wouldn't it be nice if that little girl has a relationship with the man? I'm glad you were able to convince Allison to tell the truth, Samantha."

"I'm not sure how much influence I had. Allison planned to tell Bella the truth when she was older. I also visited with my old friends, Jody and Erin. Those are two very bitter women."

"Their problem is they like the same men."

"You are observant, aren't you, Patsy?"

"I'm a born snoop. That's why I majored in journalism. I like prying into other people's business," Patsy laughed. "You'd be surprised how much information the people in town are happy to share."

"You say they like the same men. Are you talking about Will Logan?"

"Not only Will and C.J., but Ted Blanchard is on that list."

"Ted, the father of Jody's boys? He had a thing with Erin too?" Samantha said in disbelief. "How did I not know what was going on right under my nose?"

"Give yourself credit, Samantha; you weren't in town when they were feuding over Ted and Will. From what I've heard, Jody was in love with Ted Blanchard when Erin, still fuming over Jody's betrayal with C.J., set her sights on Ted and won him over. Jody discovered she was pregnant, and Ted said he'd marry her. Erin raised the roof and Ted, the coward, skipped out on them both. I guess curiosity about his son brought him back to Ashville. Jody stupidly slept with him again and, boom, another baby. Erin knew that Ted was the father of those boys but it didn't stop her from chasing after Ted. Being true to form, Ted left town again. I don't think he's been heard from since.

"Will arrived in Ashville when his company opened an office here. He and Erin met when she worked as his real estate agent. She fell in love with him and he seemed to care for her too. That's when Jody stepped in and snatched the poor guy away. I've heard Jody and Will are not the happiest couple in the world, although Will is a wonderful father to the boys."

"Now I understand why they're at each other's throats," said Samantha. "When I talked to them earlier, each hinted they had wanted to kill C.J. Maybe I'm reading too much into their ranting."

"Have you spoken to Kate Turner?" asked Patsy.

"Not yet. I plan to stop by her house in the morning. Kate wasn't as close to the group as the others. Nick was her only interest in high school, and she didn't have time to do things with her friends. After a while, we stopped inviting her to join us."

"Nick had a promising career in football, from what I understand," said Patsy. "He wasn't as good as C.J., but he did help the team win the state championship two years in a row. Thanks to those wins, he received a full scholarship to the university. I know I sound cynical but he did benefit from C.J.'s death."

"Are you suggesting Nick had something to do with the accident? That can't be; he was devastated when it happened. Nick lost his best friend that day."

"Samantha, I'm not suggesting anything, I'm just making an observation. If I hadn't received those letters, I wouldn't be questioning anyone's motives. Someone wants answers and I'd like to know why."

"I know, Patsy, you're right to investigate. I just don't want to face the possibility that someone I've known all my life is a killer."

*****

Ryan walked into the room, interrupting their conversation. He announced that the window was in place and the nail holes were repaired.

"It looks as good as new," he said.

"Come sit down; let me get you and Jim a cold beer. I can't thank you enough for fixing it so quickly."

"We're not done yet; Jim's getting his industrial-strength vacuum. That thing will pick up any glass that's embedded in the sofa and carpet. Then we'll take you up on that beer."

*****

Patsy and Samantha watched the machine work. Patsy would be careful walking around her living room barefoot for a while.

Afterwards, Jim accepted a beer but said he couldn't stay long. He and his wife were meeting friends for dinner.

"I think you know them," he winked at Ryan. "It's your boss, Al Beardsley, and his wife Marian."

"You know Coach? He's a great guy, and the reason I applied for a job here in Ashville."

"Al and I go back some years. We played football together at Ashville High; he was better than me. In fact, he was better than anyone on the team. We're lucky to have him as a coach."

"I'm surprised he didn't go on to the college level," said Patsy. "From what I hear, it isn't for lack of offers."

"I've heard that too. He doesn't talk about it much but I understand he doesn't want to move his family around. He says, as long as Ashville wants him, he'll stay here," answered Jim. "Ryan, I guess that's not so good for you."

"When I interviewed with Coach, he let me know his job wouldn't be opening up anytime soon. We agreed that this would be a stepping stone. I plan to learn everything I can from a great coach and then move on."

Patsy's heart sank at the thought of Ryan leaving town. She'd only known him for two days, but knew she wanted to go on seeing him for the rest of her life. *I'll worry about that when the time comes,* she thought to herself.

*****

Samantha drove home, thinking about her new friend, Patsy. She saw the disappointment in her eyes when Ryan talked about moving on. There was no doubt in her mind that Patsy would follow Ryan wherever he went.

*****

Her mother met her at the door. "Hello, dear. I'm happy you're home. I just got off the phone with George Sinclair. He and Sharon weren't able to get a flight tonight, but will be arriving at the airport tomorrow morning at nine o'clock. They will rent a car and be here a little after ten. Sharon said he wanted to get in his car and drive here tonight, but she convinced him otherwise. I hope he's not disappointed."

"Mom, if I wasn't certain Allison was telling the truth about Bella, I would never have suggested you call George. I'll let Allison know; do you mind if they meet here?"

"Of course not; will you be here too?"

"I'll be here if Allison wants me."

Samantha called her friend to let her know George Sinclair was anxious to meet Bella.

"I'll be honest with her, Samantha. I'll have to take her out of school to meet Mr. Sinclair, so she will know something is up. I'll tell her she's meeting her grandfather, and warn her he might not believe me and she'll have to be ready for his rejection. I hope you will be there. Bella likes you and it will make it easier for me if the man turns his back on us."

*****

Samantha called her old friend Kate.

"Samantha, it's good to hear your voice. I was hoping you'd be able to stop by the house. Is eight o'clock tomorrow morning too early?"

"Eight will be perfect; I'll come with donuts from *Dandies*. I haven't had one since I left town."

After jotting down directions to Kate's house, Samantha ended the call. She heard her father and Jack Fletcher returning home from their golf game. Her mom and Nancy had prepared dinner and she was famished.

CHAPTER 13

Samantha could hear light drops of rain against the window in her bedroom. She sat bolt upright until she realized it was still three days until the wedding. *Surely it will stop raining by then.*

Despite the dark skies, she bounced out of bed thinking about Fletch. She knew he planned to work this morning, but by late afternoon, he would arrive in Ashville. She knew his parents would want to spend some time with their son, but hoped to have him all to herself for a little while tonight.

After a shower, she pulled her hair into a ponytail. There were wonderful aromas coming from the kitchen, meaning her mother was making blueberry muffins, Samantha's favorite.

"Good morning, Mom," Samantha said when she walked into the kitchen, "You know how to make a gloomy morning seem like the sun is shining. The smell of your muffins wafted up the stairs and into my bedroom."

"I could always wake you up with my blueberry muffins when you were a teenager," Colleen laughed. "You've been so busy since you've been home; I wanted a chance to chat, just you and me this morning."

"I'm sorry, Mom; I've been preoccupied with my old friends. They have all had their share of troubles."

"Poor Allison, she hasn't had an easy time of it. Her father was a tyrant and her mother is an odd duck, to put it mildly. I hope we did the right thing by telling George about Bella."

"You do believe Bella is his granddaughter, don't you, Mom?"

"I do, and he believes it's possible. Otherwise, he wouldn't be coming here to meet her."

Mother and daughter talked for almost an hour before Samantha had to leave to get to Kate's by eight o'clock.

*****

Kate opened the door to her friend. "Come in, Samantha; what do you have there?"

"These are Mom's blueberry muffins. I know I promised donuts, but my mom makes wonderful muffins."

"They smell delicious. Your mother always was a great cook. We used to like to go to your house because she always had something wonderful baking in the oven."

"I'm afraid that talent ended with her. I'm not a very good cook, but Fletch wants to marry me anyway."

"I can't wait to meet him; your mother told my mother he's a terrific guy and nothing like Bobby Rooney."

"Didn't anyone like Bobby? I haven't heard one nice thing said about him since I came back to town," said Samantha.

"You were in love back in high school; he had a mean streak that you couldn't see."

"I guess I was blinded by love back then," Samantha laughed. "My eyes were opened the other day when he came to see me because he needs a wife to help in his political career."

"He wanted to marry you, Samantha? That's hilarious. I'm sorry, I shouldn't make fun of it and maybe you don't think it's funny."

"It's funny and pathetic at the same time. He's an egomaniac; maybe he always was and I just didn't see it."

They finished their muffins and Kate suggested they have another cup of coffee in the living room.

The room was very comfortable with overstuffed chairs and a large sofa. The fire was blazing in the fireplace, on a rainy morning, making the room even cozier. Samantha noticed a large, white Bible on the coffee table with an ornate gold cross on the front. Samantha didn't remember Kate coming from a particularly religious family.

"You noticed our family Bible," Kate said as she walked into the room carrying a tray with two cups on it.

"I was admiring it; it's quite beautiful."

"It's one of the few things I wanted from my grandmother's home. It reminds me of her. She used to read from it daily. I can't say I do that, but it makes a nice conversation piece. She and Grandpa received it as a wedding gift."

The friends talked until it was time for Kate to leave. "It's been so wonderful talking with you, Samantha. I wish we could do this more often. Any chance you'll be moving back to Ashville in the future?"

"I don't think so, Kate; my life is in Lancashire now."

"You could write anywhere; maybe Fletch could join the police force here?"

"I don't think he'd like that; Lancashire is a small enough town for him. He started his career in Chicago; you can imagine what an adjustment it was for him after leaving that environment. I will plan to visit more often, though. Between school and work, I'm afraid I've neglected my hometown long enough."

Samantha drove the short distance to her mother's house. She wanted to be there before Allison and Bella arrived.

She was happy to see Kate again although something seemed off. She couldn't put her finger on it, but Kate acted nervous, as though she wanted to tell Samantha something but couldn't get it out. They hadn't talked about C.J. The other day, Kate had said she didn't want to talk about him, and Samantha couldn't help but wonder why.

A strange car was in her mother's driveway. Samantha pulled around it and went into the house.

George Sinclair stood up from his seat on the kitchen chair and gave Samantha a hug.

"I can't believe it, after all these years. You were a beautiful little girl, Samantha, but look at you now. You're a knock-out," he said.

"Mr. Sinclair, you always were a flatterer."

"What's this Mr. Sinclair? Call me George. I'd like you to meet my wife, Sharon. Sharon, this is little Samantha, who isn't so little anymore."

"It's a pleasure to meet you, Samantha; I hope we aren't intruding on your time with your folks. Your mother tells us you're getting married this Saturday."

The doorbell rang. Everyone froze knowing it was Allison and Bella.

"I'll let them in," said Samantha.

She opened the door and saw a look of panic on Allison's face.

"Hello, Miss Samantha, my mom and I are here to see my grandpa."

"Come right in; everyone is in the kitchen." Bella looked up and saw a huge man standing in the doorway. He walked slowly toward her and she smiled broadly.

George Sinclair was well over six feet tall; he was a large man with white hair. He had a kind face and smiled easily. The sadness Sharon had seen in his eyes when they'd first met had all but disappeared. He looked at the little girl before him. His eyes filled with tears, and he squatted so that he was face to face with her. He stared at her and said nothing.

"Mom says you might not want to be my grandpa," she said solemnly.

"I would like nothing better than to be your grandpa."

"I can arrange for a DNA test, Mr. Sinclair," Allison said with a calmness she didn't feel.

"There will be no need for that; I know Bella is C.J.'s daughter without any test. She has her grandmother's eyes."

Sharon reached into her oversized purse and pulled out an album Frances had kept with photos of C.J. through the years and handed it to Allison.

"I thought Bella would like to see these pictures of her father, the resemblance is remarkable."

Allison slowly turned the pages of the album, her eyes filling with tears.

"This could be Bella when she was a baby. Trudy Mason, the woman who adopted her, always sent me copies of photos."

"There's no denying Bella is C.J.'s child," said Sharon. "Bella, why don't you come with me and we can look at these pictures together. It will give your mom and grandfather a chance to talk."

"I'd like to, Mrs. Sinclair."

"I'll go in the kitchen with you; we'll be closer to the cookies I baked this morning," Colleen said. "Samantha, would you like to join us?"

"Please stay with me, Samantha," Allison pleaded. "You don't mind, do you, Mr. Sinclair?"

"I don't mind at all," he answered. "Sharon told me you gave Bella up for adoption and finally adopted her yourself. I wish I'd known your predicament. C.J.'s mother and I would've helped you. I'm heartsick and ashamed that my son behaved the way he did. Did he know about the baby?"

"Yes, sir, I told him. He refused to believe me or believe the baby was his. I take responsibility for the pregnancy. My home life was miserable and I'm afraid I confused infatuation with love. I knew it was wrong to give myself to C.J., but I don't regret bringing Bella into the world."

"It won't make up for C.J.'s conduct, but Sharon and I would like to help you and Bella financially. I understand you're living with your mother. Is that by choice or necessity?"

"I'm not asking for any money from you. I'm a police officer and the pay is ample for our needs. We live with my mother because she's not able to live on her own."

"I'm sorry; I offended you and I never meant to do that. I won't offer it again, but if you're ever in a bind, you know where you can find help."

George Sinclair admired the young woman who had given birth to his only grandchild. He knew from Sharon's reports of conversations with Colleen that Allison Jennings' life was not easy. Bella appeared happy and well-adjusted. However, according to Colleen, she was also a troubled child.

"I'm afraid," George began, "Frances and I were responsible for C.J.'s selfishness. For the longest time, we didn't think we would be blessed with children. When Frances did become pregnant, she was very sick and was bedridden from her fourth month until C.J. was born. The doctor told us there would be no more babies. We accepted that C.J. would be our only child and doted on him from the beginning.

"Everything came easily to C.J. He had good looks, brains, and an above average athletic ability. He'd been approached by a scout for a professional football team. He told him there was no need for him to go to college. He guaranteed a place on the practice team the year he graduated from high school.

"Frances and I had always given the boy too much freedom to make his own choices and then it came back on us. He'd been recruited by four different colleges and promised a full scholarship in three of them. It was a dream for Frances and me, but C.J. had other ideas.

"We were insistent he attend college and, if at the end of four years, he still wanted to be a professional football player, we wouldn't object.

"The last time we saw our son was the day he slammed out of the house after another argument and cooled off by hiking on the cliffs. That was the day our lives ended too. Frances was never the same. I suspect she blamed me for the accident, although she never said it aloud."

Allison touched the older man's hand. She felt a terrible sadness for this family who wanted nothing but the best for their only child.

*****

Bella came bouncing into the room.

"Mom, look at this picture of my dad," she said with pride. "The football team is carrying him on their shoulders. He was a hero, wasn't he Grandpa?"

"Yes, Bella," George said. "Your dad was a football hero. Your grandmother and I were very proud of him too."

"Here's another picture of him standing next to his bike. What's that all over his pants and his socks?"

"I remember this. C.J. was about your age. His mother didn't like it when he rode his bike to the cliffs. She thought it was too dangerous for a boy his age. The day this picture was taken, he had taken a shortcut through the field near the cliffs instead of riding on the path. He came home and his pants and socks were covered with burs from the burdock plant. His mother knew right away where he'd been. She had done the same thing when she was a girl and her parents caught her because of the burs that clung to her clothing."

"I think all of us got caught riding through that field," said Samantha. "Allison, you weren't with us the day we all rode our bikes to the cliffs. I fell and when I got up, those little burs were covering me. The girls tried picking them off, but there were so many, they didn't get them all. They hurt when they stuck to your skin. When I got home, my mom knew exactly where I'd been."

"I see that look in your eyes, Bella," said Allison. "Don't even think of riding your bike to the cliffs."

George glanced at is granddaughter. "Please don't go near the cliffs, Bella."

Bella could see the sadness in his eyes. "Don't worry Grandpa, I won't," she smiled.

CHAPTER 14

Samantha watched as the Sinclairs and the Jennings walked to their cars. They planned to meet for dinner that evening. Samantha invited the Sinclairs to come to the wedding on Saturday and they accepted.

"Bella is nothing like I imagined," said Colleen. "She's a sweet little girl."

"Finding out C.J. was her father made her day. Allison said her attitude changed the minute she told her. I'm happy Allison came clean with her. The poor girl thought nobody wanted her, no wonder she acted out."

"George is beaming, isn't he?" Colleen said. "I'm sorry Frances didn't know about Bella before she died. She would have loved that girl. Sharon will be a wonderful step-grandmother. She and George make a good pair. It's sad that they both lost their spouses but how nice they found each other."

"You are such a romantic, Mom. That's why I love you so much. Speaking of romantic, I hear Fletch's car pulling into the driveway."

Samantha didn't wait for him to come in the house, she met him outside and threw her arms around him.

"I'm glad you came early. I've missed you more than you know."

"I missed you too, Samantha. That's why I'm here. The captain tells me I was worthless and booted me out of the office. Where can we go to be alone?"

"I'm afraid it must wait; Mom and Dad are watching from the window and your parents are on their way. How about a rain check?"

"I don't see a cloud in the sky, but I'll take that rain check."

"I booked us in a motel outside of town, that way we can have our privacy," Samantha winked.

"Did your parents object?"

"No, Mom reminded me that she and Dad have five kids, so she understands."

Samantha and Fletch walked arm in arm to her waiting parents. Colleen welcomed Fletch with a hug and Archie shook his hand. Sandy and Jack arrived within minutes, anxious to greet their son.

"Don't they make a wonderful couple?" asked Colleen; it was more of a statement than a question. The proud mothers couldn't stop smiling. Archie and Jack talked about their golf game and tried to persuade Fletch to join them for eighteen holes on Saturday.

The men chuckled as their wives shook their heads.

*****

"You two run along. I know you have people you want Fletch to meet," said Colleen. "Sandy and I have plenty to do before the rehearsal dinner tomorrow night."

"I feel guilty leaving you two with all the work, Mom."

"Don't be silly; we make a good team and we're having fun. Your fathers will help too."

*****

"Our folks are getting along well; I'm glad they chose to have a picnic in your backyard instead of a fancy dinner in a restaurant."

"They knew we wanted a casual affair. The reception will be low-key even though it's in the hotel. Tomorrow will be fun with all our brothers and sisters and their families. Mom invited all my old friends from school. They can't wait to meet you."

"They want to meet me to compare me to your old boyfriend, Robby or Snobby, whatever his name was."

Samantha laughed. "His name is Bobby although Snobby fits him better. He goes by Bob now and he wanted me to dump you and marry him."

"What?" cried Fletch. "When did you see this guy?"

"I saw him the other day; he's in town to visit his folks and to look for a wife. He will be running for Congress and needs a doting woman by his side."

"Should I be worried?"

"Hardly, the guy is a pretentious jerk. He might be at the wedding because Mom invited the town, including his parents, but I doubt it. A casual wedding doesn't sound like his style."

"Maybe he's the one who threatened your *lovelorn* friend. We can uncover a sinister plot and sabotage his political career before it starts."

"Why, Detective Fletcher, do I detect a hint of jealousy?"

"Was it only a hint? I thought I was being obvious."

"Let's change the subject; just the thought of Bobby Rooney is making my skin crawl.

"My lovelorn friend is Patsy Burke. I can't believe her transformation since our high school days; she's an attractive, self-assured woman now. I know you'll like her. She met the school's assistant coach, Ryan Hartman, when we were together the other day. I wish you'd seen the sparks fly between them. I do believe it was love at first sight."

Samantha had told him over the phone about Patsy and the incidents of threats made against her.

"I'd like to see the letters she received, although that's not possible."

"They weren't really letters, just a few words typed on paper. Patsy wrote the words in her notebook."

"I'd like to see what she wrote; do you think she'd meet with us?"

"I'll give her a call."

Samantha called her friend's cell phone; Patsy was working from home that morning and waiting for Ryan to stop by on his lunch break.

"Of course, you can come over, Samantha; I'm dying to meet your detective."

*****

The couple arrived at Patsy's house in less than a half hour. Ryan's car was in the driveway.

Fletch and Ryan hit it off immediately. They had a love of football in common.

"Samantha, he's dreamy; aren't we lucky to have such great guys and good-looking ones too?"

"Sounds like it's going well with you and Ryan."

"It's going better than well if it weren't such a small town, he'd be living here. We must be careful because of his teaching position. He's talking marriage. I know it's too soon for that, but it's not too soon to know I love him and want to spend my life with him."

"Patsy, I'm so happy for you. I'm glad we stopped by the school that day. We went to check out C.J.'s *shrine* and you fell in love."

"Tell me about the meeting between Allison and Mr. Sinclair. Was it awkward for her and Bella?"

"Not at all. Mr. Sinclair fell in love with Bella the minute he saw her. Her resemblance to C.J. is remarkable. There isn't a doubt in anyone's mind that she's his daughter. Allison offered to have a DNA test done and Mr. Sinclair told her it wasn't necessary. Bella has changed overnight; she's a happy little girl. Mom says she's back to her own, sweet self again. Mr. Sinclair had tears in his eyes when he looked at his granddaughter. They will be staying for the wedding and have invited Allison and Bella to visit them in North Carolina before the summer ends. Sharon Sinclair has grandchildren Bella's age. I'm happy for all of them."

*****

"Fletch, here's my notebook with the words in the letters. I wish I'd made copies of them, but I didn't think of it at the time."

"Thanks, Patsy; do you mind if I make a copy of this?"

Samantha knew the words on the paper meant something and he would mull them over in his mind until he figured out their meaning.

*****

Allison called from the police station wondering if Fletch had arrived in town yet.

"I thought he'd like to come down to the station and check out how we do things in the big city," Allison laughed.

"I'm sure he would love it; how are things going with Bella and Mr. Sinclair?"

"George, he asked me to call him George, has been wonderful. Bella has transformed back to being my sweet girl. George and Sharon picked her up from her summer class and are going to the high school to see C.J.'s display. Bella is proud of her father. I just hope she still feels that way if she finds out what a cad he really was."

"We're with Coach Ryan now. Is someone there to let them into the school?"

"Yes, Coach Beardsley is there waiting for them. Coach and George are old friends."

*****

On the drive to the police station, Samantha asked Fletch if the words on the paper meant something to him.

"I'll give it some thought; there's something familiar about the words, but I can't put my finger on it."

*****

Allison showed Fletch around the station. The other officers knew of Fletch's reputation as a crime solver. They were impressed when Allison strolled through the offices with him. Their condescending attitude had changed when they'd took turns sitting with her during Bella's hospital stay. She was one of them now even though she was a female.

"It's a small system, but seems to run well. What made you go into law enforcement, Allison?"

"I worked in dispatch while I went to classes at the community college. To be honest, I didn't want to be like my mother. I love her dearly, but she was a doormat. She had no skills other than cooking and cleaning. That wouldn't have been a bad thing, except my father was a tyrant and Mom couldn't escape him. I didn't want to be dependent on a man; I took some courses in law enforcement. I found I liked it and applied at the police academy."

"Allison, do you mind if I ask you some questions about your father?"

"No, in fact, I've thought of him and his penchant for violence since C.J.'s accident has been in question."

"I'm sure Mom never had an outgoing personality. She was still in high school when she met my father. He was an imposing man, large in stature and towering over my mother. For some reason, she fell for him and married him the day after she graduated. To my knowledge, he never struck her or harmed her physically. He didn't have to, I can still remember the look he'd give me when I did something he didn't approve of. He rarely yelled at me, but he would take it out on my mother.

"I wasn't allowed to date, so when C.J. looked my way, I was captivated. He was gentle and kind, the exact opposite of my father. He changed when I told him I was pregnant. I can remember his words were, *what do you want me to do about it? It's not my kid.* I was crushed. My mother was beside herself. If my father had found out, she knew he would blame her.

"There was never a question in my mind that I wanted to have the baby and keep it. I told Mom I would quit school and we could move out of our house. I'd get a job and she could take care of the baby during the day. Of course, that was a dream. I was only a kid, we'd be living in a tent somewhere. Back then, I didn't know about women's shelters. If I did, I might have gone to one, with or without my mother. That didn't happen and I was forced to give Bella up for adoption.

"I don't think my father knew about the baby but I'm beginning to wonder if he found out somehow and fought with C.J. on that cliff. Father was bigger than C.J. and could have easily pushed him to his death."

"How did your father die, Allison?" asked Fletch.

"He had a massive heart attack. I didn't think he had a heart at all, but it turns out he did. He collapsed out by the shed at the back of our property. Mom won't go near that shed since it happened.

"You know something, now that I think about it, she didn't have any qualms about the shed until the agoraphobia hit."

"When did that happen?"

"It was about five years ago. Bella had been with us for about a year. Mom walked her to school every morning and met her in the afternoon. One day her teacher called me at the station. She told me Bella was waiting for her grandmother to walk her home. We only lived two blocks from school and Bella knew the way, but she was worried about Mom. She was afraid if she left the school grounds, her grandma wouldn't be able to find her.

"I left the station to pick her up. When we arrived home, there was Mom, sitting on the sofa watching television. She didn't have an excuse for not walking Bella home, but to my knowledge, she didn't leave the house again until Bella was in the hospital the other day. I thought she might have had a stroke. I couldn't convince her to see a doctor and, finally, gave up trying.

"It surprised me to learn Mr. Krause had gotten her out of the house. It was only walking around the back yard, but it was a step. He did tell me she wouldn't go near the shed and panicked if he walked her toward it. I have never been inside the shed. I always associate it with my father. He spent a lot of time in there alone. Maybe it's time I bit the bullet. Will you go with me, Samantha?"

"Of course. Fletch will be with us too. Do you think your mother will object?"

"She's in no position to object. The house is in my name. Dad signed it over to me two days before he died. It was the last mean trick he played on my mother. The man was despicable."

*****

On their way to Allison's house, Samantha called her parents.

"Hi, Mom. I hope you aren't holding dinner for us. Fletch and I are tied up."

"Oh, my darling, we understand the lovebirds want to be alone. Don't worry about us. You two enjoy yourselves; there's plenty of food in the refrigerator when you can untangle yourselves."

"Mom, did you start happy hour early today?"

"Just a tad early. The boys are firing up the grill..."

Samantha could hear gales of laughter in the background.

"Don't let them burn the house down, Mom. I'll talk to you later. Don't have too much fun without us."

"They're burning the house down? It sounds like they're all drunk. That's a fine example to set for their children," Fletch laughed.

"They're having fun. Mom could never hold her liquor; she'll be sorry in the morning."

*****

"What do you think is in the shed? A dead body? A *Playboy* magazine? Maybe the old boy lined the walls with centerfold pictures," suggested Fletch.

"Yuk, I remember Mr. Jennings. He scared me to death. Thank heaven, Allison didn't take after him. I think he hated kids. What a difference between him and George Sinclair."

"Allison seems all right considering her parents."

"When I first came to town a few days ago, she was resentful and unpleasant. She was furious when Patsy started asking questions about Bella. She hadn't told Bella the story of her birth, and Allison was afraid Bella would find out from someone else. Once she told her, however, everything changed. Bella was thrilled that C.J. was her father. Allison has carried that burden around with her for years. Her parents didn't make her life easy, that's for sure.

"Turn right on the next street. Allison's house is the third one on the left."

Allison pulled in the driveway a few minutes later.

"Sorry," she said. "I had a phone call just as I was leaving so I'm running a bit late. I called Mom on the way here and she's expecting us."

*****

Mrs. Jennings opened the front door with tears streaming down her cheeks.

"I've kept quiet all these years because I didn't want you to know what your father was capable of, Allison."

Allison put her arm around her mother's tiny, quivering shoulders.

"Mom, please don't upset yourself. Fletch and Samantha are here to see the inside of the shed. Is that what you're worried about?"

They all walked into the modest but attractive living room where they saw Mr. Krause sitting on the sofa.

"Hello, girls," he said, offering his hand to Fletch. "Frederick Krause, Detective."

"Joseph Fletcher, everyone calls me Fletch. It's a pleasure to meet you, Mr. Krause."

"Mrs. Jennings asked me to be here. I'm afraid I don't know what it's all about; she told me *it's time to reveal the secret*. Martha, everything will be all right; please tell us what has you upset."

"Please, everyone sit down. I won't be able to talk with all of you standing over me."

Martha Jennings began to pace, the words forming in her mind.

Samantha patted her friend's shoulder, she could tell she was anxious about what her mother was about to say. Finally, she blurted out:

"Allison, your father killed C.J. Sinclair. The proof is in the shed out back."

Allison closed her eyes. She'd thought that might be the case, but hearing her mother confess that her father had killed the father of her child made her sick to her stomach.

"May we see the proof, Mrs. Jennings?" asked Fletch.

Martha Jennings led the way to the shed. Her step was lighter and she held her head high as she walked to the shed near the back of the property. She reached into the pocket of her dress and pulled out a key, opening the rusty lock without a problem. The shed smelled musty but was neat and orderly. Samantha noted there were no centerfold photos adorning the walls. Fletch noticed it too and gave her a slight smile.

"Back there in the corner is a box with Herbert's overalls and boots. They are covered with clinging burdock and blood. The fields by the cliffs are filled with burdock plants. They are almost impossible to get off clothing; they are also on the inside of Herbert's boots. If you look behind the box, you'll see a shovel; it has blood on it too."

"Mom, do you think Father found out about Bella? Who would tell him and how would he know C.J. was her father? Nobody knew that, not even you."

"I don't know how he found out, but it's obvious he knew and he killed that young man."

"Allison," said Fletch, "is it possible to run tests on these items to check the blood type?"

"Yes, I'll get them to the lab right away. Do you want to come with me?"

Mrs. Jennings brought a sheet from the house to wrap the shovel in and a large plastic bag for the overalls and boots.

"I'd like to wait for the results with you, Martha," said Mr. Krause.

Allison was grateful; she didn't want to leave her mother alone, although she seemed calmer than she'd been in years.

CHAPTER 15

The lab tech knew Allison and liked her. He had other pending orders, but put them aside while he ran a blood analysis.

"How are you doing, Allison?" asked Samantha.

"Not so great when I think of telling Bella her grandfather killed her father. I will not lie to her again. If it turns out that's what happened, I'm going to tell her the truth."

"I don't know the condition of C.J.'s body, but those pants and shovel were covered in blood. It indicates a vicious assault. If C.J. was beaten and thrown over the cliff, the authorities would have noticed blood on the cliff and would have investigated it as a murder, not an accident."

"I hope you're right, Fletch; the man was a horrible human being, but I hope he wasn't a killer. I feel bad keeping you from your family. I'm sure they want to be with you every chance they get."

"Don't worry about our folks, they're enjoying themselves. By the sound of the commotion I heard in the background, I'd bet Samantha's dad was serving martinis."

"I can't imagine your mother being tipsy," said Allison. "She was always so nice to your friends growing up. I loved my mom but she never had any fun. Your mom used to sit down on the floor and play games with us. She's a neat lady."

"Your mother will calm down now that her secret is out, Allison. You know from experience what a burden it is to carry around secrets."

"I also know how good it feels to have everything out in the open. Mr. Krause's friendship is good for her."

"It's good for him too," said Samantha. "Mom tells me he's lonely without Mrs. Krause. Maybe you'll have a new stepfather soon."

"Not a good visual; I can't imagine my mother hopping in bed with a man."

"I could see the twinkle in Mr. Krause's eyes," laughed Fletch. "The old guy's still got what it takes."

"What do you think, Allison? Does Detective Fletcher have that twinkle in his eyes?"

"He does every time he looks at you, Samantha. You'd better marry the guy soon."

The lab tech came out with his report.

"I'll have this typed up and get it to you. I know you are anxious for my report. I found two blood types on the shovel. One is a dog and the other, I'm guessing, could be from a coyote. I might be wrong about the coyote, but I know they're prevalent in the area near the cliffs. I can tell you with certainty that there's no trace of human blood on the shovel, the overalls, or the boots. I hope that helps, Allison."

Allison threw her arms around the older man. "Pete, you've made me very happy. Thank you for doing this for me."

"Did you have a dog, Allison?" asked Fletch.

"No, we didn't, but there was an old stray that followed Father around. He called him Butch. He was a mean dog who growled when he saw me. I used to call him Daddy's little boy because they were so much alike. Of course, I never said it to Father; I wouldn't risk his wrath."

"One day he was there, wandering around the backyard watching every step Father took and the next day he was gone. I didn't care and soon I'd forgotten all about him."

"Sounds like Butch tangled with a coyote and lost," said Fletch. Maybe we should go to the cliffs and see if we can find a grave of some kind. It may reassure your mother that her husband wasn't a murderer."

"Would you mind? It's very pretty up there during the summer."

*****

They stopped at the only discount store in the area and bought oversized hunting socks to slip over their shoes and lower legs to catch the burdock.

"Why didn't we think of this when we came up here years ago. We can throw the socks away and not have any of those pesky little things clinging to us," said Samantha.

It only took a few minutes of traipsing through the brush until they came upon a crude wooden cross with the name *Butch* etched into it. Nearby they found the bones of an animal with its skull shattered.

"Rest in peace you nasty old dog; you were a mean thing, but my father loved you. I'm sure he grieved the loss of his only friend." Allison felt sympathy for the man for the first time in her life.

*****

"It's beautiful; I can understand why your friend, C.J., liked to come here."

"They've talked about clearing the field and building a park, but the town won't consider it without adding a fence along the cliff. I can see their point for safety reasons, but it would be a lovely place for a picnic," said Allison.

"What are you thinking, Fletch? You have a funny look on your face."

"I was wondering why C.J. fell. You say he came here often to walk along the cliff. He must have known it well, so what happened that day? Did he have a dizzy spell? Did he have a sudden illness? Could it have been drugs or alcohol? Did someone meet him up here and help him over the side?"

"It's a mystery, but let's get back to Allison's and reassure her mother that it wasn't her husband who killed C.J."

*****

Frederick Krause and Martha were sitting on the front porch sipping blackberry wine. Allison was surprised to see her mother outside and she'd never seen her drink anything but tea and water.

"What did you find out, dear?" Mrs. Jennings asked anxiously.

"Mom, do you remember Butch, the dog who used to follow Father all around?"

"Yes, whatever happened to that dog? Is he still around?"

"No, he's dead and buried in the field by the cliffs. Apparently, he was attacked by a coyote and killed. We're guessing Father beat the coyote with his shovel. Those were the only two blood types on the any of the items you found."

"Are you saying your father wasn't a murderer after all?"

"That's right; Father didn't kill anyone except that coyote and the coyote deserved it."

Mrs. Jennings looked like ten years had been magically removed from her body. She smiled and turned to Mr. Krause.

"I'd love to go to dinner with you, Frederick. May we order another glass of wine when we get there?" She giggled like a school girl.

*****

"That was nice," said Fletch. "I like Allison; she's had a rough life but seems to have made the best of it. Her father sounds like a real winner."

"Yes, he was, I'm relieved he didn't kill C.J. Things are starting to work out for Allison. It would be nice if she could find a nice guy to share her life with."

"The matchmaker is at work. Tell me, what did you have to do with Patsy and Ryan getting together? Did you arrange a meeting?"

"No, I didn't know Ryan before Patsy and I met him at school; they hit it off on their own. I like them both, don't you?"

"Yes, I like them too. What about your two best friends?"

"Jody and Erin are constantly at each other's throats. They both were carrying on with C.J. at the same time. Not only that, they each think the other murdered him. I didn't think they were this bad in high school. They aren't pleasant to be around. Kate simply acts strange. I think she's happily married, but who knows? I'm glad I went away to school; if I'd stayed here I might be just like them."

"Who didn't C.J. hook up with? I always wondered what it would be like to be a chick magnet."

"You could be a chick magnet; you don't give anyone the opportunity. I'm not complaining; I like having you all to myself."

"I like having you all to myself too; let's ditch the parents and go directly to the hotel. We'll order room service and have our dinner and dessert in bed."

"It sounds wonderful, but we have to show our faces, if only for a little while."

"If your folks are anything like mine, they'll want to feed us and ply us with drinks and keep us prisoners for hours. I want to be alone with you."

"One drink and then we leave, I promise."

*****

When they entered the house, Samantha noted that her mother and Sandy were drinking iced tea. Eating a full meal had helped calm the effects of the alcohol.

"The children are here," cried Colleen. "You must be famished, I'll fix plates for you, and we have plenty."

"That sounds great, Colleen," said Fletch. "I grabbed a hot dog on the road earlier and I'm starving now."

Archie Degan handed Fletch a cold beer that went down a little faster than Fletch intended.

"What have you two been up to today? Have you been hiding in your motel room all this time?" Jack Fletcher asked with a sly grin.

"Jack!" cried his wife. "Leave the kids alone."

"No, Dad, that's where I wanted to be, but super sleuth, Ms. Degan is on her way to solving another murder."

"Samantha, please be careful. I don't know why you involve yourself in these matters," Colleen said. "I know you have been suspicious of C.J. Sinclair's accident since you arrived in town. Poor Patsy might have been killed because of her investigation. I wish you'd leave it alone."

"Mom, we did find out today that Mr. Jennings didn't kill C.J." Samantha told everyone what they'd discovered earlier and the burden of secrecy Mrs. Jennings had lived with for the last few years.

"I'm glad for Allison and Bella that he didn't do this horrible thing. Mrs. Jennings' mind must have snapped when she suspected her husband was a murderer. Let's change the subject before the Sinclairs arrive. Did I tell you we invited them over after they dropped Bella at home?

"That reminds me, Samantha, Erin Shaw called earlier and asked if she could bring a guest to the wedding. I told her it would be fine. I hope that's all right."

"That will be great, maybe with someone to keep her company; she'll forget her feud with Jody for a while," said Samantha.

"May we add one more name to the list?" asked Colleen. "Sharon Sinclair's son is coming to town. I asked her to bring him along."

"This was supposed to be a casual wedding with just a few people," cried Samantha. "What is Sharon's son doing in Ashville? He's never lived here."

"Sharon's son is an attorney," replied Colleen. "He's afraid Allison is after George's money and he's coming to check out her story. Sharon hasn't told George the reason for his visit, but I suspect George has figured it out."

*****

"We'd better get going, Fletch; it'll be a busy day tomorrow. I, for one, need my beauty sleep."

"You two run along and enjoy your last night together until you are officially married."

"What do you mean, our last night? We have tomorrow night too," said Fletch.

"No, you don't son," said his mother. "It's tradition for brides and grooms to be apart the night before the wedding. Samantha will be sleeping here tomorrow night and you won't be able to see her before the ceremony."

"It's a stupid tradition if you ask me," Fletch grumbled.

*****

They were in the motel room in less than five minutes. Samantha freshened up in the bathroom after a tiring day and when she walked through the doorway to the bedroom, Fletch was sprawled on the bed sound asleep. She slipped under the covers beside him, kissed his forehead and fell asleep immediately.

CHAPTER 16

"Fletch, wake up! It's almost nine o'clock. We're due at my parents' in thirty minutes."

Startled, Fletch said, "What happened to the night?" Did he really fall asleep? The thought of making love to Samantha all night long had kept him going during the three-hour drive to Ashville. Now there wasn't time this morning and tonight she wouldn't be sleeping with him. This day wasn't starting out well.

"Why don't we stay here and order breakfast in bed?"

"Our parents have planned a special breakfast for us. Breakfast in bed sounds wonderful but we're in Ashville. There's no room service anyplace in town. I could probably find some stale donuts and a weak cup of coffee in the lobby if you'd prefer that to Mom's blueberry pancakes, bacon omelets, perfectly fried hash browns, piping hot coffee and homemade raspberry Danish."

"Your mother's cooking wins. Let's shower together; it will save time."

"You think so, huh? Maybe we'd better not start something we don't have time to finish."

*****

Colleen and Sandy were awake before dawn preparing for breakfast. The Degan's dining room table wasn't large enough to accommodate the number of people invited to brunch. Luckily, it was a sunny, warm day. Archie and Jack set up borrowed tables and chairs in the back yard.

Samantha and Fletch's siblings and their families would be at the party. George and Sharon Sinclair were coming, along with her son, Matthew Benson, and Allison and Bella.

Samantha was surprised they made it on time. Her hair was still wet from the shower, but she pulled it into a ponytail and the warmth of the day was already drying it. Samantha hugged her brothers, sisters-in-law and nieces and nephews. She'd met Fletch's sister before, but not his younger brother. Samantha sat next to Allison to help her feel more comfortable with so many strangers.

Allison whispered to her, "Matthew keeps staring at me; he thinks I'm trying to con George."

"Why do you say that?"

"Sharon told me he's an assistant district attorney in North Carolina. I get the feeling he doesn't trust Yankees."

"He's cute, isn't he?"

"Unfortunately, he knows it. I don't like him."

"If he's here to check you out, he'll realize you and Bella aren't trying to swindle anyone. I'll ask Fletch to reassure him."

"No, don't; I don't need anyone to vouch for me. If he wants to distrust me, that's fine. I just don't want him interfering with the relationship Bella and George are beginning to form. I'm tempted to stick my tongue out at him; isn't that mature of me?" Allison laughed.

*****

Mimosas and bloody Marys were served along with apple juice for the younger set. The atmosphere was relaxed with everyone talking and laughing. Most guests were strangers when they arrived, but made friends quickly. Bella and Dennis Degan's daughter, Kelli, strolled by the pond behind the Degan house.

They were talking about boys and clothes when Matthew Benson approached.

"Hello, Bella. I'm Matt Benson. My mother is your step-grandmother, Mrs. Sinclair. That makes me your uncle."

"That's so cool. I never had an uncle before."

"What do you know about your dad?" Matt asked.

"My mom says his name is C.J. Sinclair. His real name is Chandler James, but nobody knows that except Grandpa and me. There's a statue of my dad in the high school. He was the best football player in Ashville. He died when he fell off the cliffs. Mom says I shouldn't go there because it's dangerous."

"Does your mom tell you a lot of stories, Bella?"

"She used to read me stories from library books, but now I read them myself."

"Bella," cried Allison when she spotted Matthew Benson talking to her daughter, "the other kids are looking for you and Kelli. I told them I'd send you back to the house."

"Okay, Mom; did you know this is my Uncle Matthew?"

"I suppose he is." Allison shuddered at the thought. When they were alone, she looked Matthew in the eye. "I don't want you upsetting my daughter. She's just a child. If you have something to say, say it to me."

"I would never say anything to hurt a child. I only wanted to hear what Bella had to say about this cockamamie story that she's George's granddaughter. I'm sure you know George is a wealthy man. I'm only concerned that a ten-year-old granddaughter suddenly appeared in his life."

"I don't see where it's any of your business. I have kept Bella's parentage a secret for reasons that seem unimportant now. George Sinclair and Bella have formed a special bond in a very short time. I have not asked George for money and I don't intend to. I don't care if you believe me or not; I'm not a con artist."

"What in the world is going on here?" George's voice boomed as he approached the couple. Sharon looked nervously at her son; she knew he could be a hot-head and didn't want him disrupting the party.

"George, just what do you know about this girl?" Matthew asked. "Doesn't it strike you as odd that she suddenly presents you with a half-grown grandchild?"

"Matthew, you aren't interrogating a witness on the stand. I've known Allison since she was younger than Bella is now. Although I hate to admit this, my son was not a nice young man. He took advantage of Allison and when she discovered she was pregnant at fifteen-years-old, he refused to help her. Allison's life has not been easy; I offered to help her out financially and she refused. If you compare Bella with photos of C.J., you would know Allison is telling the truth.

"Look," he continued, "I know you're Sharon's son and I have great affection for you, but I'm telling you now to mind your own business."

"I'm sorry, sir; I was only trying to protect you."

"Do I look like I need protection? I'm not as feeble as you seem to think."

"You're not feeble at all; I was out of line. I hope you'll forgive me, and I hope Ms. Jennings will accept my apology."

"There's no need to apologize, Mr. Bennett," Allison said. "I only ask that you leave me and my daughter alone while you're in Ashville."

Allison didn't trust this man and liked him even less than she did when he'd been scowling at her earlier.

*****

"What's wrong with you, son?" asked Sharon. "Whatever happened to the boy who always showed compassion for people? This job has made you bitter. Now, let's go join the others with smiles on our faces."

Matt Benson didn't like being chastised by his mother; suddenly, he felt eight-years-old again.

*****

Fletch sat next to his mother. "We haven't had much time to talk since I got here," he said.

Sandy patted him on the arm. "I miss you, Joey; we don't get to see you nearly as often as we'd like. I'm happy Samantha is in your life. She's a wonderful girl and she loves you; a mother knows these things."

As they talked, little Timmy Degan ran in front of them and tripped on his shoelace. His chin quivered as Fletch picked him up and tied his shoe.

"Timmy, this is my mother, Sandy."

"Hello, Timmy."

"Hello, Miss Sandy. My Aunt Samantha is going to marry Uncle Fletch and they're going to have a bunch of babies."

"A bunch, huh?" said Fletch. "How many is a bunch?"

"Lots of 'em."

"Do you go to school, Timmy?" asked Sandy.

"I go to Sunday school, but only on Sundays."

Sunday school thought Fletch. *That's it!*

"Mom, you'll have to excuse me; I need to get something from my car."

Samantha watched him walk quickly around the house; she was curious but was having a conversation with his sister and didn't want to stop her in mid-sentence.

CHAPTER 17

Fletch pulled his notebook from his briefcase and entered the information into his computer. *I knew it sounded familiar; I don't know why it took me so long to figure it out.*

"I'm going to find Fletch," said Samantha. "He's been gone for over ten minutes; I hope it isn't the station calling."

Samantha saw Fletch sitting in the car with a strange look on his face.

"Everything all right, sweetheart?" she asked.

"Yes, come in and sit with me."

Samantha opened the door; the windows were rolled down, but it was still hot in the car.

"Samantha, did I ever tell you I was a chronic liar when I was a kid? I told big lies, little lies, stupid lies. Any kind of lie there was, I told it."

"You're not lying about wanting to marry me?"

"No, of course not; I said when I was a kid. Well, my grandmother lived with us for the last few years of her life. She was a retired school teacher who had also taught Sunday school for years. I can remember her sitting in her rocking chair every night reading her Bible.

"My parents punished me for my lies, but nothing worked until Grandma took over. Every time I told a fib, she would force me to memorize three or four verses from the Bible that talked about lying. She wouldn't let me leave the house until I recited the passages flawlessly. I can tell you, I missed a lot of baseball practices that summer."

"Patsy gave me a list of the words in the letters she received. I've checked every one and they're excerpts from bible verses. This one is from Proverbs 12:19: *Fruitful lips endure forever, but a lying tongue is but for a moment.* Whoever wrote it only included the part that mentioned lying: *but a lying tongue is but for a moment.*

"That narrows it down to someone who reads the Bible, or at least, has one in their home," said Fletch.

"Oh my," said Samantha. "Kate Turner has a beautiful old Bible on her coffee table. It's a family heirloom given to her by her grandmother."

"Was she sleeping with C.J. too?"

"Not that I know of, but I didn't know about the others either. Kate and Nick Turner were together through junior and senior years. They've been married several years. If C.J. hadn't died, Nick probably would be just another high school football player. Instead, he received scholarships for college."

"Have you seen either of them since you've been home?"

"I spent time with Kate on two occasions. She came to Mom's the first day I was home. Jody and Erin were there and talked about C.J. Kate didn't like the conversation and insisted we change the subject; she seems agitated when C.J.'s name was mentioned. I wonder if she discovered Nick had something to do with the accident."

"Let me think about this for a while; we don't know if Kate's Bible had anything to do with these letters," said Fletch. "Maybe we should rejoin the party. Your dad will be accusing me of seducing you out here on the street."

*****

I misjudged Allison Jennings, Matt Benson thought to himself. *Everyone seems to like her. She doesn't look like a gold-digger; in fact, she's a fine-looking woman, fine-looking indeed. If I haven't blown it, I'll see if I can make amends with a Mimosa.*

Matt grabbed two Mimosas from the bar on the patio.

"Go get her, Matt," said Archie Degan.

"I'm going to try, Archie," he replied.

Allison was standing with Sharon Sinclair. Matt was certain his mother was defending him.

"A peace offering," he said as he offered the drink to Allison.

"No thank you," she replied, turning her head away.

"Mom, how about you?"

"No, son, I've had enough, for now; you'll have to drink them both yourself."

"Did I tell you I don't like champagne and I like orange juice even less," he said.

"Maybe you should have thought of that before you took two glasses. Are you always this presumptuous?" Allison asked.

"Never more than twice a day," he answered.

"I'm going to leave you two to battle it out; I don't want to watch my son lose his case," said Sharon, giving him a wink.

"Has my mother been telling you I'm really a nice guy?" he asked.

"She's been telling me all sorts of things about how lucky she is to have four wonderful children and one pompous ass."

"She was talking about my brother. Are you ever going to forgive me?" he pouted.

"There isn't anything to forgive, not that I liked being the subject of your disdain, but I do understand you were trying to protect your mother's husband from my greed."

"Would you like to take a walk down toward the pond; I just saw a fish jump out of the water."

"I love watching them go after bugs in the air. I hope it was a mosquito; it will be one less that bites Bella today."

"She's a sweetheart; let's see, if she's my sister, what are you to me?"

"Well, let's see, you and I aren't blood relatives, so we are sorta in-laws. Because my daughter is your step niece, it would make me your step-sister—if I had married C.J. You don't already have one of those, do you?"

"No, but but it sounds totally crazy," he laughed.

"You might as well know, I have a very dysfunctional family. My mother is nothing like yours. We won't even talk about my father and you've probably guessed that I was barely older than Bella is now when she was conceived. Yes, it's crazy, but that's my family."

"We don't have to talk about your family if you don't want to. You seem to have overcome any obstacles in your way, Mom says you're a police officer; that's terrific."

"This is Ashville, not exactly a high crime area, most of my cases involved auto accidents and hauling drunks to the pokey on a Saturday night."

"Are you involved with anyone?"

"No, Bella has been my life for the last six years. It's a long story; I'm sure you don't want to hear the details."

"I'm a good listener if you want to talk about it."

Allison found Matt easy to talk to. She told him all about C.J. and her foolish infatuation, about the adoption and finally getting Bella back, her father's abusive behavior and her mother's mental illness. She half expected him to turn and run by the time she'd finished her tale of woe. Instead, he wrapped his arms around her and held her tight.

*****

Bella played happily with the other children. She was on the brink of womanhood, but behaved like a child at times. She spotted her mother and Matt standing by the pond. Matt had his arms around her.

It had only been two days since she'd found out her real dad was C.J. Sinclair and now her mother was hugging someone else. Bella quietly broke away from the other children and walked the four blocks to her home.

The latch on the side door of the garage was loose. Bella easily opened the door. She hopped on her bike and rode the mile to the cliffs where her father had died.

Mom will be mad if she finds me here; I won't stay long; I just want to tell my dad that he's my father.

*****

Allison felt comforted in Matt's arms. She wasn't in the habit of pouring her heart out to anyone, especially a man. Kelli Degan startled her when she ran up and struggled to catch her breath.

"I can't find Bella anywhere, Ms. Jennings. We were playing with the other kids and she disappeared. Do you know where she went?"

Allison asked if she'd gone inside the house to use the bathroom.

"No, she's not in the house; I looked everywhere."

Allison glanced toward the pond. Matt could see the terror in her eyes.

"Okay, everyone, we have a missing child in the area; has anyone seen a pretty little girl named Bella?"

The search began, none of the other children saw Bella near the pond; the small inflatable boat was still tied to a tree. Archie had intended to store it safely in the garage and away from adventurous children. He was too busy making sure he had enough vodka for bloody Marys and forgot to hide the boat.

Colleen and Samantha, who knew the house best, searched every room including the basement but found no sign of Bella.

"Maybe she went home," said Allison. "Kelli, did Bella talk about getting something from her room to show you?"

"No," said Kelli through her tears.

Allison walked to her car, George and Matt followed.

"You're in no shape to drive a car, Allison," said Matt. "Point me in the right direction and I'll get you there."

"You aren't going without me," said George. "I didn't discover my granddaughter only to lose her again."

*****

Mrs. Jennings was sitting in her favorite chair when the three of them walked through the door.

"Mom, is Bella here?"

"No, dear, Bella's with you. Did you know Mr. Krause took me dancing last night? He's a very nice man. Do you know Mr. Krause?"

It was obvious to Allison that her mother had reverted to another world again. She couldn't deal with it now. She had to find Bella and called her name.

"I saw Bella on her bike. She rode in front of the window. She didn't wave goodbye."

"Thanks, Mom. You sit tight; I'll be back in a while. I'm going to look for Bella."

Allison walked through the garage door where Bella's bike was stored. "Her bike is gone," she cried.

Matt wondered if Bella had seen him comforting her mother. He would never forgive himself if something happened to Bella because of his actions.

"I don't know where to start looking for her," said a distraught Allison.

"Do the kids still sneak over to the cliffs?" George asked quietly.

"Bella knows it's dangerous; I don't think she'd go there," said Allison.

"That's where her father died, isn't it, George?" asked Matt.

George dropped his head in his hands. "Do you think she went there to be close to her father? Death is very confusing to a child."

Matt drove Allison's car through the brush to within a few feet of the cliff drop off. Allison spotted Bella's bicycle.

The sound of the car doors opening surprised Bella; she turned quickly and lost her balance.

"Bella!" Allison shouted when she saw her daughter slip on the rocks.

Matt ran to her and realized that one wrong move on his part and the girl would drop to the bottom of the ravine. He was glad he'd worn rubber sole shoes, otherwise, he could easily have slipped himself.

Bella looked up at him, her eyes pleading for help.

"Stay very still, Bella. I'm going to move slowly toward you," he whispered. "I want you to grab my hand as tight as you can."

Bella did as she was told. She looked directly into Matt's eyes. He looked nice; she liked his face. Maybe it would be okay if Mom liked him too.

Allison and George stood by helplessly as Matt inched his way down the cliff. Allison held her breath when she saw Bella's hand take hold of his. He slowly brought her to safety and to the arms of her mother.

George held out his hand helping Matt to his feet.

*****

"Bella, darling, why did you come here? You know it's dangerous."

"I wanted to talk to Dad; I didn't mean to slip. Thanks for saving me, Uncle Matt. Grandpa, did you know Matt is my uncle?"

"I know that and I'm glad to hear it. Your family gets bigger every day." He hugged his granddaughter and said a prayer, thanking God she was safe.

After returning to the party, Allison led Bella away from the crowd to a bench tucked away under the trees.

"Why did you go to the cliffs, Bella? Did it upset you when you saw me with Matt?"

"At first, it bothered me; I've never seen a man put his arms around you like that. I thought you might leave me like my other mom did. I wanted to talk to my dad. Maybe his spirit is still on the cliffs. Do you think that's true?"

"Your dad's spirit lives in George's heart and in here," Allison said, pointing to Bella's heart. "Matt had his arms around me because I told him about giving you up when you were a baby and getting you back. I always cry when I talk about being without you for those first years and he was comforting me."

"Matt likes you," Bella said with a big smile.

"I hope he likes me; I like him too." Allison could feel the warmth in her cheeks and hoped Bella didn't notice.

"Matt really likes you. I think he loves you."

"Bella, we just met this afternoon. We don't know each other well. He lives in another state, and I won't see him after Samantha's wedding tomorrow. Love needs time together to grow. It doesn't happen right away."

"You said you loved me the first time you saw me."

"That's a different kind of love; I carried you inside me for nine months before you were born. That gave me plenty of time to know I loved you.

"Why don't you join your friends, they look like they're having fun."

*****

As Allison walked to the pond, she heard Samantha call her name.

"Hey, girlfriend, George told me about Bella and her scare; is she all right?"

"She's fine; I shudder to think what might have happened if Matt hadn't been there. He saved her life."

"It looked like you two were getting along well," Samantha grinned.

"After a rocky start, he turned out to be a nice guy."

"If he's anything like his mother, he's a sweetheart. I'm happy George found Sharon. I loved Frances like a second mother but she's gone and George deserves to be surrounded by grandkids. His eyes light up when he's around Bella."

"She loves him too," Allison said. "The party's winding down. I heard your father say something about cook-out tonight. It's a good thing you don't get married every day.

CHAPTER 18

Megan and Mike and the rest of their Lancaster friends arrived in the early afternoon. The wedding participants met at the chapel to rehearse for the next day. After the rehearsal, everyone gathered again in the Degan backyard. Colleen and Sandy were busy most of the day preparing food for the rehearsal picnic, as they called it.

The mimosas and bloody Marys were replaced with beer, wine, and any drink Archie and Jack knew how to concoct.

"What's with our folks?" asked Fletch. "They've become party people in their old age. Listen to the music they're playing."

"They're having fun; let them enjoy our day. We will have plenty of time to be alone."

Allison and Matt walked toward Samantha and Fletch. "Guess who just strolled in and look who she dragged with her. That woman is a troublemaker."

Samantha turned to see Erin, walking arm in arm with Bobby Rooney.

"Erin, Bobby, so nice of you to join us," she said, smiling. "Mom said you were bringing a friend."

"We want to meet your detective, Samantha. I heard he's dreamy and he certainly is."

Samantha felt a chill pass through her when she looked into Bobby's cold eyes. Why did she ever think she was in love with this man?

Fletch stepped forward and introduced himself to the twosome. "Help yourself to a drink or some food; there's plenty of both."

"I see your father is pouring drinks, Samantha; is the bartender on a break?" Bobby asked sarcastically.

"My father *is* the bartender, Bobby; we're just simple folk, remember?"

Samantha could feel his eyes on her as the couple walked toward the bar. "I used to think Erin was the sweet one and Jody the bitch; now I'm not so sure."

"Erin has become very bitter. Jody isn't any better. They both need to grow up," said Allison

Samantha felt Fletch's hand on her back and as Erin and Bobby headed to the bar, he said, "Have I told you how sexy you look standing over here by this big tree? Do you think anyone would notice if we hid in the bushes and made out?"

"What a great idea; I wonder if Dad has cleared out this year's crop of poison ivy."

"On second thought, how about a drink?"

"That sounds safer; do you realize in less than twenty-four hours we'll be married."

"Are you sure you want to marry me? That Rooney guy thinks he'd make a better husband than some lame cop."

"I don't care what that Rooney guy thinks; I'm sorry, I didn't know he'd be here. He's an old regret from the past."

"You don't need to apologize; we've all had relationships that we'd like to forget. Did he tell you he's running for political office?"

"Yes, and he wants a little woman by his side. Erin is perfect for the part."

"Which one has the Bible on her coffee table?"

"Kate Turner," Samantha answered. "She and Nick are standing over there. I'll introduce you."

They walked toward the couple not realizing they were arguing.

"You started it," Nick said.

"I told you I was sorry," Kate answered. "Nick, I wish you wouldn't drink so much; it doesn't help you forget what happened."

Nick looked up and saw Samantha and Fletch walking toward them and nudged Kate's arm.

"Hello, Samantha," he slurred his words slightly. "Hello, Detective; I'm Nick Turner and this is my wife Kate."

"Please call me Fletch. It's good to meet you and all Samantha's friends."

"I wish you could have met C.J. Sinclair," said Nick. "He was a helluva great athlete; he would've made it to the pros, you know, he was that good. What a waste; he's dead now—he was good, really good and great even."

"Nick, we'd better get you home," said Kate. "The heat mixed with alcohol isn't good for him. It was nice meeting you, Fletch. We'll be at the wedding tomorrow."

Kate declined Fletch's help getting her inebriated husband to their car.

"She was anxious to get him out of here before he said anything too incriminating," said Samantha. "Did he sound like a guilty man?"

"Maybe not guilty of murder, but he's hiding something. Was he a drinker in high school?"

"I don't know. Those football players always took good care of their bodies."

*****

Patsy and Ryan arrived with Coach Beardsley and his wife. Marian.

"Sorry we're late, Samantha; nothing can interfere with a coaching meeting."

Samantha knew Patsy was controlling her temper. Everyone thought Coach Beardsley was such a wonderful man, but he worked his players and Ryan way too hard in her opinion.

The men gathered around Coach and Ryan to hear their predictions for the upcoming football season. Marian Beardsley saw some of her friends from the hospital auxiliary and joined them, giving Samantha and Patsy time to talk alone.

Samantha filled Patsy in on the argument the Turners had had before Samantha and Fletch had interrupted them. She told her about the old Bible on Kate's coffee table and Fletch's theory about partial bible verses on the letters Patsy had received.

"That does make sense, doesn't it? But how would we prove it was Kate who sent them? If Nick is involved in a murder or a cover-up, why would she want to call attention to C.J.'s death?"

"I'd like to talk to Kate in private, but I don't know when I can with the wedding tomorrow."

"I'm sorry I got you involved in this; maybe we should leave it alone. Whatever we find out won't bring C.J. back and we could be destroying lives in the process."

"I agree with you, but then I look over at George Sinclair. He lost his son and deserves to know how he died."

"Who's that with Allison? She looks happy."

"That's the new Mrs. Sinclair's son, Matthew. He's had a busy afternoon. He saved Bella from falling off the cliffs and into the ravine and he's responsible for the smile on Allison's face. Things are turning around for her. Her mother seems better and her father is no longer a suspect in C.J.'s death. Best of all, she told Bella the truth about her birth and the little girl has made a complete transformation. George Sinclair took one look at Bella and fell in love with his granddaughter. He told my dad he wants Allison and Bella to move to North Carolina. She would if she didn't have to worry about her mother."

"You show up in town and everyone is falling in love. I saw Erin with your old beau, Bobby Rooney. Now that's a match made in heaven," Patsy laughed. "Wouldn't it be nice if they married and she moved to Washington with him? Jody might have a chance at happiness if Erin wasn't around to spoil things for her."

"Did I hear my name mentioned?" chimed Jody.

"We were just saying what a nice couple Erin and Bobby make," said Samantha.

"I agree; wouldn't it be nice if they married and she moved to Washington with him?" replied Jody.

"That's what Patsy just said." They all laughed.

"What's so funny?" said Erin, joining them, and obviously on her third or fourth martini. "Your new guy is very cute, Samantha; you'd better watch out or I might grab him. I don't mind your leftovers."

"You're welcome to my leftovers, Erin, but Detective Fletcher is mine and I'm not sharing him."

"We'll see about that," Erin said as she sauntered over to Fletch. "Hello, big fella, I'm Erin; remember me?"

"Come on, Erin, it's time to go," Bobby said.

"But I'm having fun, Bobby; just one more drink."

"We'll have it at the hotel."

He dragged her to his rental car. *He'd marry her on the condition that she stick to wine from now on. How could he win an election with a drunken wife?*

*****

The party continued into the early evening. Samantha looked around at the empty plastic cups and plates.

"Mom, it's a mess and we have a wedding tomorrow."

"Your father hired a clean-up crew. He promises me they'll have the yard back in shape quickly. Almost everyone is having a good time. Poor Erin, I've heard she likes her vodka a little too much. She might be more than Bobby Rooney can handle. I do feel bad for Kate and Nick Turner. Nick was always a nice boy; I've never seen anyone change so drastically. He hasn't been the same since high school."

"I'd almost forgotten what Nick was like before C.J. died," said Samantha. "We thought the change was because he lost his friend. Do you suppose it's more than that?"

"What are you saying? Do you think Nick might have caused the accident?" asked her mother.

"It's possible any one of my classmates might be responsible for C.J.'s death. Still, it could have been nothing more than a tragic accident."

*****

Samantha watched as Fletch and Ryan were in a deep conversation about football with Coach Beardsley. Samantha couldn't remember Coach's first name, although she'd heard it before. He was referred to as Coach even by those who'd never touched a football or baseball bat in their lives.

Samantha wondered when Coach's hair turned snow-white; maybe he was older than she thought, or maybe he was simply aging prematurely. Amber, his daughter, was old enough to hold down a part-time job working for Patsy on the newspaper. She thought about C.J.'s funeral and how Coach's wife had consoled her husband whose emotions had gotten the better of him.

She could feel her cell phone vibrate in her pocket. She wasn't expecting calls, but turned her ringer off.

She thought it might be Megan verifying the time she and Matt would be arriving in Ashville the next day.

Samantha was surprised when the caller ID showed Kate Turner's name.

"Hi, Kate; is everything all right?"

"Samantha, I know the party is still going on, but is it possible you and Fletch can break away to come here for a few minutes?"

Samantha knew by the sound of her voice that something was wrong.

"We'll be there in five minutes, Kate."

*****

Fletch didn't ask any questions; he and Samantha drove to the Turner house without an explanation to the party guests who kept on partying.

Kate opened the door. It was obvious she was crying.

"I'm sorry to take you away from your party. Nick has something he wants to tell you. He and I can't live with the secret any longer."

Samantha and Fletch walked into the living room. The antique white Bible was on the coffee table. Nick was staring into space. His eyes that had sparkled as a teenager were moist and dull; he had a look of despair on his face and his shoulders slumped.

He looked up and said almost in a whisper, "C.J. committed suicide and it's my fault."

With that confession, he broke down and sobbed. Kate held him in her arms while nine years of tears he'd bottled up spilled out.

Samantha and Fletch sat in silence until Nick regained his composure.

"Suppose you tell us the story, Nick," Fletch said sympathetically.

CHAPTER 19

"C.J. and I were like brothers. My folks moved to Ashville when I was eight-years-old. It wasn't easy being the new kid in school. I hated my father for making us move; I missed my friends and hated my new school. Most of the kids just stared at me that first day. I wanted to sit at my desk during recess but the teacher made me go outside. I stood by the fence and watched the other kids play and never felt so alone. C.J. walked up to me and asked if I wanted to play ball with the guys.

"C.J. was only a kid and already he showed promise of being a great ball player. We played football every day after that. In the spring, we changed to baseball; I was good at both, but he was better.

"I know the kids thought I was jealous of him, but I wasn't. In so many ways he made me a better player. He was certain to win a scholarship to Stanford or Southern Cal or any one of the best football colleges in the country.

"The week he died, we were in the biggest game of the year. We were playing East Hamilton High. Their team had won the national championship the year before and almost every one of their players were juniors and returned to the team as seniors. C.J. and Coach were well-known and expected to pull off a victory. It was only a high school football game, but the interest was wide-spread.

"After practice one day that week, I waited for C.J. in the parking lot. He usually went to the cliffs to walk and calm down after an intense practice. I wanted to ask him about a play he and Coach were talking about.

"A couple of guys drove on the lot. They approached C.J. when he walked out the door. I thought they were going to mug him and I walked toward them. There were several teachers' cars and trucks in the parking lot and they didn't see me coming. When I walked closer, their voices became clearer. I couldn't believe what I was hearing. They handed C.J. an envelope and he took it. I tried to tell myself it was meaningless, but I knew, in my heart, C.J. had taken a bribe to throw the game that week.

"I waited until the goons pulled out of the parking lot before I confronted C.J. He didn't deny he took money to fix the game. He showed no remorse and said it was only a high school football game and it was easy money.

"I struggled all night debating whether to tell Coach about the money or protect my friend from his own greed. I told myself I was morally obligated to tell Coach the truth. It also meant C.J. would be off the team making me the starting quarterback.

"I was still debating my dilemma when I ran into C.J. the next morning. He walked down the hallway with a defiant swagger almost daring me to tell his secret. I took him up on that dare and went directly to Coach's office.

"I saw the crushed look on Coach's face. He insisted there was another explanation for the exchange of money. I didn't think Coach believed me and was sorry I'd told him.

"C.J. was in the habit of walking on the cliffs. He had done it many times before and knew the rocky path very well. I don't believe he fell accidentally; I think he jumped because of what I did."

*****

A sense of relief came over Nick; he buried his head in his hands. Kate held him close as she spoke.

"Samantha, you guessed I was the one who wrote the letters to 'Dear Patsy.' I had no idea 'Dear Patsy' was the mousy girl from school. Ever since C.J.'s death, our lives haven't been right. Nick was a carefree teen until then. At first, I thought the change in him was simply grief over losing his friend. Not that I expected he would get over C.J.'s death, but after a time he should have come to grips with it because life does go on. It wasn't until after we married that he told me his part in the incident. No matter what I said, I couldn't convince him that C.J. was the one who'd decided to take a bribe and ultimately jump off the cliff.

"The guilt has taken over Nick's life. He blames himself and it's getting worse; he admits to drinking too much, too often. We planned to have a couple of kids by now, but I can't bring a baby home to a father who refuses to get help for his depression.

"The Bible sits here on the coffee table and I found myself looking up passages about truth. In desperation, I wrote those bible passages hoping 'Dear Patsy' would print them and bring the sordid mess out in the open."

"Do either of you know anything about Patsy's mishaps?" asked Fletch.

"I know about the accident; I've heard the authorities suspect someone tampered with her brakes," answered Kate. "Nick didn't know anything about the letters and I can assure you, I didn't rig her brakes. I wouldn't know how to do it."

"Did you know she was knocked down and her purse taken with the letters inside? Patsy was on her way to the police station when it happened. Her purse was returned to her with everything intact except the letters."

"'Dear Patsy' took me seriously?" cried Kate. "My instincts were right about her."

"You didn't change your mind and decide to retrieve the letters, did you, Kate?" Fletch asked firmly.

"No, Fletch, I swear I didn't. I only mailed a handful of them and thought they were ending up in the trash, so I stopped sending them altogether."

"You and Patsy were the only two people who knew about the letters you'd sent," said Samantha. "You didn't mention them to anyone?"

"No, I felt foolish; it was a childish thing to do. "We'd better get back to the party; I hope we'll see you two tomorrow," said Samantha.

*****

"What are you thinking, Fletch?" Samantha said on the drive back to her parents' house.

"Nick Turner has needlessly tortured himself all these years. He was no more responsible for C.J.'s death than I am. My gut tells me C.J. didn't kill himself. I've known guys like him; they think they're superior to the rest of us and wouldn't think about depriving the world of their existence. I don't buy the accident theory either. Nick said he knew those cliffs well and I believe it. I'd like to talk with Coach Beardsley and ask him if he talked to C.J. about the bribe? Was C.J. suspended from the team and probably from school?"

"Good idea and I'll ask Patsy if there's any possibility someone might have seen those letters."

CHAPTER 20

The party was still in full swing. Samantha smiled when she saw Allison and Matt together; they made a nice couple. A long-distance relationship might not be ideal but it wasn't impossible.

Bella was happily playing with all the children. Samantha marveled at the change in the girl in just a few days. Finding out the truth about her father had made the difference. She would do what she could to find out how C.J. had died.

Fletch found an opportunity to speak with Coach Beardsley. Coach was reluctant to talk about C.J. and Fletch noted he became agitated with his questions.

"It was many years ago, son; let the boy rest in peace."

"Do you remember Nick Turner telling you he saw C.J. take a bribe?"

"Of course, I remember, but it wasn't true. C.J. had an opportunity to attend the best schools leading to a future with a professional team. After his career as a player ran its course, he had the brains to succeed in any profession he chose. He'd never risk it all for a mere five-thousand-dollars."

"Is that how much they gave him?" asked Fletch.

"They didn't give him anything. Nick Turner tried to get C.J. in trouble because he wanted to play himself. As it turned out, C.J.'s accident gave him the opportunity to do that. Why aren't you talking to him about his part in all this?"

"You're saying you never spoke to C.J. about the accusation of his accepting a bribe. Don't you think C.J. would have wanted to know what his friend told you? Wouldn't he want to offer a defense or deny the charges?"

"Look, this is a party; I'm not going to discuss the subject any further."

Coach Beardsley turned his back and headed directly to the bar. *The party won't go on forever, Coach. We will talk again,* Fletch thought to himself.

*****

Meanwhile, Samantha drew Patsy and Ryan away from the crowd.

"Is there anyone who might have seen those letters with passages from the Bible?"

"Amber, my assistant, often helps me with the mail," said Patsy. "She sorted them according to subject. I can't imagine why she'd tell anyone about those letters. They wouldn't make sense to her; they didn't make sense to me either."

"Maybe they didn't make sense to you, but they alarmed you enough that you intended to take them to the police," said Samantha.

"Samantha," said Ryan, "you don't think Amber Beardsley hit Patsy on the head and took her purse, do you? She's one of the nicest students in Ashville High."

"I'm not saying she did any of those things to Patsy, but maybe she told someone about the letters."

"Who would she tell?" asked Patsy. "Her friends were all little kids when C.J. died. Unless you're thinking of Coach Beardsley?" said Patsy.

"Samantha, you're making a mistake if you suspect Coach Beardsley of hurting Patsy. He's a tough coach, but he'd never cause anyone harm," said Ryan.

"I'm not accusing anyone, Ryan; I'm just trying to find out who wants to harm Patsy. Taking her purse and throwing a rock through her window are bad enough, but she could have been killed when they tampered with her brakes. I think you'll agree, it's important that we investigate every possibility."

"I understand. Coach has been good to me and I feel a loyalty to him. You're right, we do have to check him out. Here's Fletch; is that why he was talking to Coach?"

Fletch joined them and said Coach was hiding something. Ryan looked toward the bar and saw Coach glaring back at him. Maybe he wasn't innocent after all.

*****

The party was winding down and the guests began to leave.

"I can't believe these people will all be together tomorrow for the reception. I never dreamed the party tonight would go on so long," said Samantha.

"Okay, you two. Say goodnight," said Sandy. "Fletch, we'll drive you back to the hotel for the night. Samantha will stay here."

"I still think it's a stupid rule. They should call it torturing the groom," Fletch winked.

He gave Samantha one last kiss before reluctantly leaving with his parents.

*****

Samantha slept fitfully that night and it had nothing to do with marrying Detective Joseph Fletcher. She knew it was the best decision she'd made in her life. Her sleeplessness had to do with C.J. and his untimely death.

Nick Turner was certain C.J. committed suicide when he was caught accepting a bribe to throw a game. Because Nick was the one who'd spilled the beans to Coach, he'd suffered from regret since the day his friend died. Samantha couldn't imagine C.J. killing himself under any circumstances. She thought back to when they were children. No matter what mischief he got himself into, he could wiggle his way out of trouble. He thought he was invincible and would never have given up on his dreams. He'd often talked about his life after football. He thought he would go to Hollywood and become a movie heart-throb. C.J.'s ego wouldn't allow him to jump off that cliff.

Samantha wondered what Coach had done about Nick's accusations. Had he confronted C.J.? Everyone knew C.J. hiked the cliffs often. Did Coach follow him there? Would he have put Patsy's life at risk trying to stop her from investigating C.J.'s death? It didn't make sense. Coach was tough and expected only the best efforts from his players, but she couldn't see him risking the life of another person.

She fell asleep thinking about Coach's daughter, Amber. Amber had access to the letters 'Dear Patsy' had received. Is it possible she'd mentioned them to her father? *Coach and his family will be attending the wedding,* she thought aloud. *I'll have a talk with Amber tomorrow.*

CHAPTER 21

Samantha woke to the delightful aroma of coffee brewing. The sun was shining through her bedroom window. Despite her thoughts about murder and death the night before, she was excited. Today was the day she would marry her best friend. She didn't want to miss a minute of it and jumped out of bed. After showering, she joined her mother in the kitchen.

"Mom, are you crying?"

"Yes, but they're happy tears. I'd forgotten how much I missed you, Samantha. I know you're happy living in Lancashire, but I like to reminisce about the old days when you and I would sit right here at the table and talk about anything and everything. Today's your wedding day and I couldn't be happier for you, but I do miss my little girl."

"Oh, Mom, I miss those days too. It's been wonderful being home this week, although I have been preoccupied with C.J.'s possible murder."

"Do you really think he was murdered? If it's true, I'm glad Frances never knew the truth. She believed it was an accident; it would have been so difficult for her if he'd been purposely killed. Who do you think is responsible?"

"I have a theory, but no proof. I'll talk to Fletch about my suspicions this morning. He might have some ideas."

"Samantha Degan, it's your wedding day; why not concentrate on your happiness and put talk about murder aside."

"All right, Mom. I'll think only wedding thoughts," she lied.

"Megan and Mike will be arriving shortly. I'm glad you asked her to be your maid of honor. Mike seems like a nice young man. I hope he's good enough for her after her last boyfriend, Jimmy Lee Butler. I cringe when I think of how he terrorized you."

"Mike's the greatest; I wouldn't be surprised if they tied the knot soon."

*****

Fletch knew he wasn't allowed to see the bride before the ceremony but his mother didn't tell him he couldn't call her.

"Hello, beautiful, are you doing anything special today?"

"Only marrying a gorgeous hunk, the love of my life, whose name has slipped my mind, but I'm sure I'll remember it when it's time to say I do," Samantha answered.

"Did you sleep well last night?"

"Not very well; it was lonely without you. I've been thinking about Amber Beardsley. Other than Kate Turner and Patsy, she's the only one who had access to the letters Kate wrote to 'Dear Patsy.' I thought you might like to help me question her discreetly."

"Wasn't she just a kid when C.J. died?"

"She was then, but she's not anymore. I don't know Coach Beardsley well, but I don't think he's the type who'd ignore Nick Turner's accusations against one of his players, especially his star quarterback."

"Do you think he fought with C.J. on the cliffs?" Fletch asked. "What about the threats to Patsy? Rigging the brakes in her car could be attempted murder."

"That's what's throwing me. I don't think he'd put anyone's life in jeopardy. If he and C.J. argued, his death wouldn't have been intentional but a horrible accident."

"Megan and Mike just walked into the hotel coffee shop; we're having breakfast with my folks. Megan said she'll see you in an hour. Mike will drop her off at your house. I can't wait to see you in the chapel."

*****

The chapel was small, but the office was big enough for Samantha to change into her wedding dress. She hoped Fletch approved of her choice. Megan brought her bridesmaid's dress with her and planned to change at the chapel too.

Less than an hour after Fletch's call, Megan arrived at Samantha's house. "I thought I was hungry but I'm too nervous to eat. How do you stay so calm, Samantha?"

"I'm not nervous at all. I know Fletch is the right one for me. I don't think it's sunk in that he will be my husband today."

"Samantha's not nervous about getting married because she's solving a crime in her mind," said Colleen, walking into the kitchen.

"Colleen, you look beautiful," Megan said. "If I didn't know better, I'd say you were the bride."

Colleen twirled around showing her knee-length dress and jacket in a teal that accentuated the green of her eyes. She was close to sixty-years-old but looked younger.

"Sandy Fletcher and I shopped together for our mothers-in-law dresses. Sandy has excellent taste, don't you think?"

"It doesn't hurt that you have the figure of a twenty-year-old," Samantha said with pride.

Her father stood in the doorway. "You do look like a bride, Colleen. Shall we have a double wedding with our daughter?" Archie laughed.

"And have everyone think we've lived in sin all these years?" Colleen smiled.

"Oh, Mom, people don't live in sin anymore." Samantha shook her head at her mother's use of an old-fashioned term.

"Samantha, I can't wait until your children are grown and make fun of the things you say to them."

"Colleen, she'll never have those children if we don't hurry," said Archie. "We don't want to keep Fletch waiting."

*****

Colleen and Megan helped Samantha get ready to walk down the aisle. Archie opened the door to the chapel office and gasped. Samantha looked so beautiful it took his breath away. He bit his lip trying to control his emotions. He was a big man and it wouldn't do to have him blubbering in front of his friends.

Colleen kissed her daughter on the cheek and left to be escorted down the aisle by her oldest son. Sandy was already seated and was blinking back tears of happiness.

The music played as Megan walked toward the altar; she only had eyes for Mike who looked more handsome than ever standing beside the groom. Mike stared at Megan thinking how lucky he was to have her in his life.

The wedding march played and Samantha walked down the aisle on her father's arm.

Fletch watched as she came toward him. It was as if the entire world disappeared and only Samantha was left in it. Her smile matched the one he felt in his heart.

The ceremony was a blur until he heard the minister say, "You may kiss the bride," and introduced Detective and Mrs. Joseph Fletcher to their friends and family.

*****

The reception was in full swing when the bridal party arrived at the hotel. The photographer Colleen had hired believed the more pictures taken, the more would be ordered and so he took them until Archie told him they had plenty to choose from.

The champagne was flowing and the bar was knee-deep in partakers. Samantha thought her father wouldn't be happy until all the alcohol in the town had been consumed. She was happy to see Nick Turner with a glass of ginger ale in his hand. He smiled and thanked Samantha for easing Nick's guilt.

Erin wasn't as wise and had a half-full glass of champagne in her hand while she clung to Bobby Rooney's arm. Bobby worked the room hoping to make himself memorable to eligible voters.

Samantha noticed Amber sitting with her family, and Patsy and Ryan. Her brother Josh's eyes were fixed on his phone. Samantha knew a boy his age would rather be with his friends than sitting around a room filled with old people. Amber tried encouraging him to put his phone down and join the other teens on the dance floor but he ignored her.

"Samantha, you look beautiful," said Patsy.

"Thanks, Patsy. I wonder if you could help me with my dress in the lady's room? Megan and Mike are dancing and I don't want to disturb them."

"Of course," Patsy said, excusing herself from the table. "This doesn't have anything to do with your dress, does it, Samantha?"

"No, I wanted to discuss Amber with you."

Samantha asked if Patsy was sure Amber was the only person in her office to see the letters.

"Amber is the only person who had access to my files. I could ask her if she told anyone about them. I'll ask her to join me on the patio. Come out when you see us there; the girl will be honest with me."

Samantha joined Fletch who was deep in conversation with his brother. He knew her plan and asked if she needed his help.

"No, it might frighten Amber if she thinks she's being interrogated."

"I hope you get the answers you need to solve the mystery. I want your full attention tonight, Mrs. Fletcher."

"Don't worry, Detective, nothing will distract me from my gorgeous husband."

Fletch felt a hand on his shoulder and heard a woman's hushed voice asking him to join her outside in the front garden.

He turned and saw Erin Shaw walking toward the door. He followed her, noticing she walked steadily for someone who'd been drinking non-stop for the last couple of hours.

"Hello, Erin, what can I do for you?"

"Fletch, you're a cop and I might need protection. I have something to show you."

Fletch was ready to make a run for it as she started to unbutton her blouse.

"It's a bug!" Fletch cried as he saw what was oh her shoulder. "Who are you recording, and why?"

"I probably shouldn't be telling a detective this, but I've been blackmailing C.J. Sinclair's murderer."

*****

Meanwhile, Samantha met Patsy and Amber on the patio.

"Amber," Patsy said, "Samantha and I have a few questions for you; do you mind answering them?"

"Sure, what's up?"

"Amber, do you remember seeing a handful of letters with bible verses about truth?"

"Yes, those are the ones you were taking to the police when you were mugged; why do you ask?"

"Did you tell anyone about the letters? Anyone at all?"

"No, I don't remember telling anyone. Wait a minute, maybe I did mention it to Mom. Was it a secret? I'm sorry if I did something wrong."

"You didn't, Amber; I never said they were confidential. Do you think your mother told anyone else?" asked Patsy.

"I don't think she even heard me. She and my brother were having another row when I told her. I heard him slam the kitchen door on his way to his friend's house. Mom says Josh is going through a phase, but he was born a jerk."

"Do you think Josh heard what you said? Do you think he'd tell your dad?" asked Samantha.

"I don't know. I'm sure he wouldn't think it was important. He acts so strangely when he's around Dad. Like I said, he's a jerk."

*****

Josh suddenly appeared on the patio. "Are you talking about me, Amber? I know you think I'm a jerk but I don't care. I can't wait until you graduate and go off to college. You make me sick."

"Josh, please, there's no reason to speak to Amber that way. We were asking her questions about some letters Patsy received at the newspaper. Do you know anything about them?"

Josh's face turned pale. He looked through the window to where his father was sitting.

Coach Beardsley knew instinctively that his son needed him and joined him on the patio. "Is everything all right here, son?" he asked.

Josh shouted. "I'm going to jail and it's all your fault, Amber. I didn't want to hurt you, Patsy. I just wanted to stop you."

CHAPTER 22

"What have you done, Joshua? Why would you go to jail?" his father cried.

"I hit Patsy on the head and took her purse; I fixed her brakes but only to scare her. I didn't want her to get hurt. I threw the rock through her window and she still didn't stop."

"Didn't stop what?" Coach asked, losing patience with his son.

"She didn't stop sticking her nose into C.J. Sinclair's accident. I was trying to save you, Dad. I saw you do it that day. I saw you hit C.J. and that's when he fell off the cliff."

Coach's mouth flew open. "Don't say any more, Joshua." He looked and saw George Sinclair staring at him.

George had stepped out of the ballroom to watch the children playing catch on the lawn.

"What's the boy saying, Al? Did you fight with my son? Are you responsible for his death?"

"I don't know what he's talking about. We're going home now. I'm not saying another word until I talk to my attorney."

Sharon held George's arm, begging him not to do anything he'd be sorry for.

"The man killed my son, Sharon; you don't expect me to forgive and forget."

"You don't know the whole story; now is not the time for retaliation. You're frightening Bella. Please calm down."

He looked over at Bella and smiled at her. He spotted Detective Fletcher and demanded Coach Beardsley be arrested.

"I'm sorry, George; I have no authority in Ashville. I'll call the police department; I'm sure they'll want to question Josh and the coach. It's not easy, but there's no way of rushing this investigation."

"Patsy watched as they drove away; she knew Amber was crying and she couldn't do anything to help her."

*****

Most of the party guests were unaware of events taking place on the patio. Allison invited George, Sharon, and Matt to her house hoping a change of scene would help George overcome his shock.

"Coach was like a second father to C.J. I can't understand why he would turn on him like that."

Allison wondered if there was more to the story, but didn't share her suspicions with anyone. She remembered the change in Nick following his friend's death and guessed he knew something he'd kept inside all these years.

*****

Patsy's phone vibrated. She answered and was surprised to hear Amber Beardsley's voice.

"Patsy, I know the reception is still going on, but are you and Coach Hartman able to break away? Josh wants to talk to you. He'd wants to talk to Detective Fletcher and Samantha too before Dad sees a lawyer."

"Ryan and I will be there, Amber. I'll ask Samantha, but there's no guarantee she and Fletch can come."

Samantha and Fletch excused themselves from the reception and joined Patsy and Ryan.

*****

Amber was waiting at the door when the visitors arrived. Coach sat on the sofa with Marian beside him. Josh was waiting at the kitchen table.

"Josh," Fletch said, "you do understand, Ashville is not in my authority, but I'm required to relay anything you tell us today."

"I understand. I want to tell what happened. Dad picked me up from school that day. It surprised me to see him because Mom was usually waiting for me. I asked him where Mom was and he said she was busy. I knew something was on his mind because he always got quiet when he was worried, usually right before a game. I sat in the back seat and didn't say a word. He didn't drive to our house; he drove his jeep through the field until he was almost next to the cliffs. I wasn't allowed to go near them, so I was excited to be so close.

"I saw C.J. Sinclair jogging along the path like he always did. Everybody in town knew C.J. All my friends wanted to be like him when they grew up. Dad stopped the jeep and walked up the side to the path. I could hear shouting, mostly from Dad but I couldn't hear what they were saying. I saw Dad take a swing at C.J. and C.J. fell.

"I could tell by the look on Dad's face that he was really mad. I didn't say anything and he forgot I was in the jeep. He drove home and I slipped out of the car and went to my room.

"After dinner, Dad got a phone call telling him C.J. had fallen off the cliff. I'll never forget the look on Dad's face when he heard the news. I was the only one who knew Dad was at the cliffs and had fought with C.J. I wasn't ever going to tell the secret and then I heard Amber telling Mom about the letters sent to 'Dear Patsy.' I knew exactly what they meant. I had to stop Patsy from taking them to the police. I didn't want to hurt her, but I couldn't think of another way to get those letters. I watched her walk out of the newspaper office and toward the police station. That's when I popped her on the head and took her purse. I didn't steal anything; I gave the purse to an old man who was walking by the newspaper office. He called me *ma'am*, maybe because my hair is long. I took the letters home and burned them in our fireplace. I know I was wrong to rig her brakes, but I just wanted to scare her, not hurt her." Josh hung his head in shame.

Al Beardsley walked into the kitchen and put his arm around his son, "I had no idea Josh was carrying this burden all these years. He's right; I forgot he was in the back seat when I confronted C.J.

"I'll admit, I was furious with my star athlete. For George Sinclair's sake, I don't want to damage the boy's reputation, but you must understand the gravity of the situation.

"One of his teammates discovered that he had accepted a bribe to throw the game that Friday night. I didn't want to lose the game, but more than that, C.J. was throwing his future away. I knew if he accepted money one time, he'd do it again.

"Everyone knew C.J. hiked the cliffs and I drove up there to try to knock some sense into him. Everything came easily to C.J.; he had good looks, brains, and tremendous athletic ability.

"I asked him if what I'd heard was true, that he took a bribe to throw the game. At first, he denied it, but I knew he was lying. I told him I'd be forced to cut him from the team, that he'd be a disgrace to his folks and the town. He shrugged his shoulders and said, *it's only a game*.

"I'm afraid my temper got the best of me. I've never hit a student in my life, but I lost control and took a swing at him. I caught him off-guard and the blow knocked him off his feet.

"I knew I had to get away from him to calm down. I told him to meet me in my office the next morning at seven o'clock sharp. He didn't answer me and I left without looking back.

"I couldn't believe it when I heard he'd fallen and was dead. I swear he was fine when I left him. I know I should have come clean when it happened, but I made the excuse that my family needed me. The truth is, I let my son believe I was a murderer all these years—maybe it's the truth. I do know I'm a coward, but I'm ready to face the consequences of my actions now."

*****

Samantha felt sick to her stomach. She'd told herself she would be satisfied when C.J.'s killer was found, but there was no sense of relief. Nick Turner and Coach had suffered the agony of guilt through the years and their families were affected by their behavior.

Samantha could smile and act as though nothing had happened. She knew lives would change. Coach would lose his job and maybe his freedom. The same with Josh; he would be punished. She didn't know how Patsy felt about the situation, but hoped she wouldn't be too hard on the boy who thought he was protecting his father.

C.J. would no longer be the hero in everyone's eyes. She couldn't believe her childhood friend had grown up to be so self-centered.

George Sinclair looked so happy with Bella sitting next to him and chattering away. He would be devastated to discover the truth about his son.

"Coach's actions are questionable," said Fletch, "but, I'm not sure he's responsible for C.J.'s fall."

*****

In another part of the room, Bob Rooney was conversing quietly with Erin.

"Erin, it's over," said Bobby. "Coach has taken the blame and you have no proof that I pushed C.J. off that cliff."

"I was there, remember?" said Erin, "I saw Coach hit C.J. and then drive away. That's when you appeared out of nowhere and taunted C.J. when he tried to get up. Finally, you shoved him hard and he went over the cliff. I wasn't close enough to make out who it was, but I know it was you."

"There's a minor detail you're forgetting; it's called proof. You have no proof and, besides, you were so drunk, you thought I was Jody. Nobody will believe you, Erin. After all these years, I've gotten away with murder once and I wouldn't hesitate to do it again."

Bobby's words and the coldness in his eyes frightened Erin. She was happy she'd only pretended to drink the champagne. She had never been more sober than she was at this moment. Why did she think she wanted a man at the cost of her dignity? She was ashamed of herself for blackmailing him into proposing. Bobby was right about one thing, she *was* a drunk.

*****

Fletch had watched the scene between Rooney and Erin from across the room. He wasn't able to hear the words, but knew when someone felt threatened and could see fear on Erin's face. He took Samantha's hand and walked toward the couple.

"Everything all right here?" he asked.

"Mind your own business, Detective," Bobby said with a clenched jaw.

Erin opened her blouse and pulled out the bug. "This should help, Fletch. Thanks for covering me."

Samantha looked in shock at her husband and then at her former boyfriend. "Bobby, what's this all about?"

Bobby turned toward the door and was stopped by a uniformed local police officer.

"Don't listen to anything she has to say," he shouted as he was led to the waiting patrol car. "She's a drunk; everybody knows that."

Erin's hand shook when she handed the bug to Fletch. "Samantha, I owe everyone an explanation. I'd like Jody, Allison, and Kate to hear what I say."

They all gathered around as Erin began her tale: "I don't know when my crush on C.J. started. I think it was in third grade. You can't imagine how happy I was when he finally noticed me. I was only sixteen, but I knew I was in love. When I found out he was also with Jody, it broke my heart and I thought I'd never forgive her. To help ease the pain, I took a few sips of liquor from my dad's liquor cabinet. I don't think it helped the pain, but it gave me the courage to ride my bike to the cliffs and watch C.J. while he jogged along the path.

"One day, I waited for him longer than usual; it was hot and I felt dizzy. Shortly after C.J. showed up, I heard a car and saw Coach get out. He ran up to the path where C.J. was jogging. They looked to be arguing but my eyes were blurry. The next thing I knew, Coach punched C.J. and C.J. fell to the ground. Coach walked back to his car and drove away.

"I started to go to C.J., but my legs were so weak, I couldn't stand up. It was then I saw someone walk to where he was and knock him down again. I couldn't see who it was, the light was in my eyes and I was dizzy from the liquor. I watched as C.J. fell over the cliff. I must have passed out, because the next thing I knew, sirens were blaring. The paramedics lifted C.J. on a stretcher and I thought he was going to be all right. Nobody saw me when I got on my bike and rode home. I didn't know until the next day that C.J. was dead and I was sure it was Jody I'd seen with him.

Erin continued, "Bobby stopped by my house after Samantha turned down his marriage proposal. He thought he could just walk back into her life and she would open her arms to him. I invited him in and poured him a bourbon; he told me he didn't think Samantha ever loved him because of C.J. He told me he'd taken care of that problem long ago. It was then that it became clear to me that it was Bobby I'd seen standing over C.J. He realized he'd said too much and I told him I'd been there and had seen what he'd done. I looked at him and the thought came to me that it wouldn't be so bad to have a handsome, powerful, and rich husband. I put my arms around him and said I would take Samantha's place. I also mentioned that a wife wasn't required to testify against her husband.

It was merely a suggestion, not a threat, but if he wanted to take it that way, I wasn't going to argue. You can see how desperate I am to have a man of my own. I'm so ashamed."

Jody was the first one to sit by her friend. "Erin, I'm sorry we've been so suspicious of each other. I want to be your friend again; do you think it's possible?"

"I'd like that, I've missed you."

*****

The party went on until long after the bride and groom left for their honeymoon.

Detective and Mrs. Joseph Fletcher were finally alone. Fletch took his bride in his arms, smothering her with kisses. Samantha forgot about everything except the love she felt for her new husband and the wonderful life they would share.

EPILOGUE: SIX MONTHS LATER

The investigation into the death of C.J. Sinclair was, once again, closed. Bobby Rooney admitted he followed C.J. that day, but that C.J. fell accidentally. Because there was a lack of evidence to the contrary and Erin's recollection was unclear, charges were not brought against Bobby. His political career was over, however. He left Ashville vowing to never return. Patsy thought Josh Beardsley had suffered enough and refused to press charges. He pled guilty to criminal mischief and was ordered to complete one-hundred hours of community service. He fulfilled his obligation in a matter of weeks.

Coach resigned his position at the high school and the family moved to a small town in California where no one had heard of C.J. Sinclair. Coach would carry the burden of striking C.J. to his grave.

Coach Ryan was offered a head coaching job in Lancashire. The 'Dear Patsy' column is syndicated now and the local Lancashire paper picked it up for publication. Patsy and Ryan were married in the little chapel in the woods in Ashville on Christmas Eve and moved to Lancashire the following week.

Allison's mother died in September. Allison sold her childhood home and moved herself and Bella to North Carolina near Bella's grandfather and near a certain attorney named Matt. Allison was quickly hired on the local police force. She and Bella love being close to their adopted family and George loves having them near. He was crushed when he was told his son had taken a bribe. He wasn't a fool and knew C.J. had many faults, but he was saddened by a life cut short. He stopped blaming Al Beardsley for the accident. He understood his frustration with the boy.

*****

After their romantic honeymoon, Samantha and Fletch moved into their new home. Samantha says it's a work in progress and will be just as they want it by July when their families come for a visit.

Megan and Mike are still going strong. She moved into Mike's apartment. Her mother calls weekly to ask when she plans to marry Mike. Megan is taking her time; she doesn't want to make another mistake like she did with Jimmy Lee Butler.

Despite everything that is going on in Samantha's life, she managed to publish another mystery.

Megan could hear her on the phone talking excitedly to her agent. She broke the connection and burst out of her office.

"Megan, they want to make *Stonehill Manor* and the professor's story into a movie. Can you believe it? They want me to fly to California tomorrow to meet with the executive producer. A movie about Professor Stonehill, my Professor Stonehill. He'll get so much recognition, I wonder what he would say if he was alive?"

"Samantha, that's terrific. What can I do to help you get ready?"

"You can pack a bag and come with me. There are two tickets in my name and I know Fletch won't be able to get away. Please say yes."

"I'd love it. I've always wanted to see California with the palm trees and the movie stars; do you think we'll see any?"

"Palm trees, maybe, but I'm not sure we'll see movie stars."

*****

Samantha called Fletch at the station. He was happy for her but detected hesitation in her voice.

"Are you nervous about the flight, Samantha?"

"No, it's not that; I was excited when Hap first mentioned the trip, but now I'm apprehensive about it. Maybe because I'll be away from you."

"You'll kick yourself if you don't follow through. Go out there and make your decision. You have good instincts." Fletch ended the call and wondered if her instincts were already kicking in. Maybe he shouldn't have encouraged her to go.

*****

The plane landed at LAX and the travelers stepped out of the terminal into the warm sunshine.

"We won't need these heavy coats here," said Megan. It's beautiful and I've had my fill of snow."

Riding to the hotel in a shuttle, Megan loved watching the palm trees swaying in the slight breeze. She watched intently hoping she'd spot a movie star.

Samantha and Megan were in high spirits, not knowing what was ahead and not realizing a murder was about to take place in Seabrook Shores.

*****

ABOUT THE AUTHOR

 Jane O'Brien is a wife, mother of three, and grandmother of five. Jane and her husband, Dave, have lived in several states in their over fifty years of marriage. They are retired and live in Northern Colorado. Jane enjoys writing mysteries and family and friendship novels. *Murder in Stonehill Manor* is the first in the Samantha Degan Mystery series, followed by *Murder in Lancashire*. This book, *Murder in Ashville*, is the third in the series.

Coming soon: *Murder in Seabrook Shores*.